BEARS
IN THE
Woods

K.C. WELLS

This is a work of fiction. Names, characters, places, and incidents either are the product of the author's imagination or are used fictitiously, and any resemblance to actual persons, living or dead, business establishments, events, or locales is entirely coincidental.

Bears in the Woods
Copyright © 2021 by K.C. Wells
Cover Art by Meredith Russell
Photos by Ben Fink Productions

Cover content is being used for illustrative purposes only and any person depicted on the cover is a model.

Chapter 1

"So, you got any questions?"

Jim Traynor turned to smile at Dave, the cheerful man who'd showed him to his cabin. "I don't think so. But if I do, who do I speak with—you, or the owners?"

Dave chuckled. "That'll be me. You'll find my number in there," he said, pointing to the large green folder sitting on the coffee table. He gave Jim an inquiring glance. "You here for the winter sports?"

Jim shuddered inwardly. Sports meant people. "No, I'm just after some peace and quiet."

Dave arched his eyebrows. "Well, you're gonna get plenty of that. This is one of ten cabins I maintain, and so far this winter you're the first guest."

This is getting better and better.

"You've got lots of places to explore, right on your doorstep. There's Pine Mountain Lake, Sonora, the Mercer Caverns, and the western gate of the Yosemite National Park is only twenty-two miles from here." Dave smiled again. "You'll be spoiled for choice."

Jim had no intention of indulging in any sightseeing, but he played nice and smiled back.

When Dave got no response, he cleared his throat. "Okay then. Time I left you to settle in. You know how to reach me if you need me."

"I do. And thank you." Jim was already ushering him to the door.

Dave paused at the threshold. "Is what I was told

correct? You're here for a month?"

"That's right."

Dave expelled a long breath. "Man, you must really love solitude."

You have no *idea.*

He stepped outside with a cheery wave, and Jim closed the door. He pushed out a sigh of relief. *Now to get a good look at this place.*

He had a mental list of requirements, and so far the cabin was ticking all his boxes. He had Wi-Fi—admittedly crappy Wi-Fi, but it would do, just about—power, and a coffee maker, so that was the work side of things taken care of. The small dining table would serve as a desk, and if he wanted an inspirational view while he worked, there was the little balcony off the living area, which looked out into the woods. That said, he'd need to wear layers, because December in Yosemite meant snow and temperatures of anywhere between the mid-forties and mid-twenties. Ever the practical man, he'd brought his own power strip with a ten-foot cord in case he needed to plug in the laptop and there wasn't an available outlet nearby. He'd even brought his own supply of coffee, because Heaven forbid he didn't like the brand of coffee the small store offered.

The living area was all done out in pine, like the rest of the cabin. There wasn't much in the way of furniture, only a couch and armchair, a coffee table, the small dining table and two chairs by the window, and a TV. Tucked away in the corner was the kitchen part, not that there was much to it, only a stove, a sink, and a microwave, plus the precious coffee maker, of course. For heating, there was a gas fireplace.

It'll do. As long as Jim had a place to work, wash, and sleep, he was happy.

He walked through the bathroom, complete with tub and shower, into the bedroom. Again, it was sparsely furnished, with a king bed, a large dresser, and a chair, but it was all he needed. *If I wanted luxury, I'd have chosen someplace else.* The cabin was simple, with a rustic charm, and perfect for Jim's needs.

He went back into the main room, opened the doors onto the balcony, and stepped outside. Jim gazed at the snow-covered trees and drew in a lungful of cold, crisp air.

It was a long way from San Francisco. Thank God.

The four-hour road trip had included a couple of stops. Yosemite was only one hundred seventy miles away, but Jim couldn't remember the last time he'd driven more than twenty miles. The route planner on his phone had tried to give him scenic points along the way, but Jim had ignored them. He just wanted to get there, and to hell with stopping at tourist spots.

Tourist spots meant *tourists*, even in winter.

Jim sighed. *I'm turning into a curmudgeon.* Then he grinned. *I can live with that.* The only people he dealt with on a regular basis were his landlord and his agent, and only then if it was absolutely necessary. If he wanted to interact with people, he did so through Gary and Mick, his amazing detectives.

Fictional characters beat flesh-and-blood people, hands down.

His stomach grumbled, and Jim went back inside to find his backpack, where he'd stowed a couple of protein bars. He still had to shop for groceries, and then that would be the necessities taken care of. Jim opened his pack and reached into it, his fingers brushing the notebook he'd brought along, its virgin pages crying out to be scribbled on as he jotted down his ideas.

Except the ideas had been a little… elusive so far.

Is this it? Is this what writer's block feels like? If so, this was a first. In ten years of writing, he'd never been stumped for ideas, but right then it felt like he was traveling through a desert, devoid of landmarks or anything else to ignite that spark of creativity he so desperately needed.

It couldn't go on like this. He had a book to finish, for God's sake. *The* book, where he'd let Gary and Mick go off into the sunset after years of solving fictional crimes. Not that there hadn't been a few battles about *that* with Valerie York, his agent. If it had been up to her, Gary and Mick would have been solving crimes well into their eighties.

Jim sank into the comfortable couch, the groceries forgotten for the moment. He couldn't blame Valerie for wanting the series to continue. After all, it had made his name—well, Dayton O'Connell's name: no one had a *clue* who Jim Traynor was. Three releases a year, regular as clockwork, and twenty of them on the *New York Times* Best Seller List.

Yeah, he could *really* see why she wouldn't want that particular gravy train to come to a permanent halt. But Jim had had enough. He wanted to write something else. Something different.

The only problem was, he didn't have a clue what that would be.

Jim pushed out a sigh. *Groceries. Writers need to eat, remember?* Not coming up with ideas would have to wait.

God, it's quiet here.

After the noise and bustle of San Francisco, the silence came as a shock. Except it wasn't silence. When he stood on the balcony, staring out into the darkness—and my *God*, it was black out there—little by little, sounds began to filter through: the wind in the trees; the hoot of owls, and the stirring all around him that spoke of (hopefully) small (hopefully) harmless creatures. As his eyes grew accustomed, Jim glanced up and caught his breath.

Oh my God, the stars.

It was as if the heavens had been strewn with dust, and every mote and speck sparkled and shone, some larger and brighter than others, all of it awe-inspiring. Jim stared at the vast canopy above him, feeling as insignificant as an ant. Then he realized that as dark as the sky was, there were darker shapes against it where no stars could be seen—the outline of the trees. Jim recalled the words of Robert Frost in his poem, *The Mountain*, and for the first time, he understood what the poet had meant.

Humbled, Jim came back inside and closed the doors. He sat on the couch, a glass of wine close by, and gazed at the laptop sitting on the table by the window. He hadn't written a single word all day, but that wasn't surprising, given how much time he'd spent on the road, and shopping, and unpacking. The real test would be in the morning.

Am I going to wake up as I've woken these past few months, dreading the day?

Jim didn't know what was wrong. He only knew that each time he sat in front of the laptop, the words wouldn't come. What was worse, all he had was the barest outline of a plot for the book, which wasn't like him. Valerie had expected to have the manuscript on her desk by now. At least her three-times-a-week calls had now been reduced to one—she'd kept that up for three weeks before obviously realizing they were having no effect. But when she'd made an offhand remark about getting away from it all to find inspiration, Jim had seen a glimmer of light at the end of the tunnel.

Getting away from it all. But from what?

That part was easy. Away from complications, bullshit, noise, and the never-ending parade of bad relationships that crashed and burned. Not *his* relationships—Jim knew better than to get caught up in such a mess—but the ones that surrounded him, invaded his space, and filled his social media. Jim had no time for *any* of them. Emotions? All they did was sap his energy. Physical relationships? He didn't need them, because any such relationship came with baggage attached, and Jim was having none of that. No, what he wanted was time to think, to breathe…

To be emptied, awaiting inspiration.

The cabin had seemed like the perfect solution. Jim had done his research, ignoring the large resorts complete with play areas for children, live music venues, lodges for dances, etc. He wanted solitude. Peace.

And as few people as possible.

When he'd first seen the cabins in Yosemite, he'd been intrigued. They varied in size, but all he wanted was something just big enough for one. Nothing too fancy—this wasn't a vacation, after all. And they were set apart, providing privacy.

Perfect.

The cabins were owned by Julian and Michael Ingram, and there'd been a photo of the couple on the website—a couple, judging by the matching wedding bands. They were a handsome pair, both in their early fifties possibly, with beards more gray than black, and piercing eyes that caught Jim's attention. He wasn't sure if they lived on site, since it wasn't mentioned, but he assumed not if Dave was maintaining the cabins.

Jim's first thought had brought a smile. *What do you know? There are bears in them there woods.* His next thought was to hope they weren't the kind of owners who were likely to drop by unannounced, just to make sure he was okay.

He sipped his wine, his attention drawn to the notebook he'd placed on the coffee table. It sat there, mocking him. He could almost hear it. *Go on—open me. Write something. I dare you.*

Jim sighed heavily. *Are all writers blessed with such overactive imaginations?* Not that he ever mixed with other writers to find out. Jim existed in seclusion. He didn't give interviews. He didn't do online posts. He didn't exist on Instagram. It hadn't harmed his sales—the public still lapped up his books—so he figured 'if it ain't broke, don't fix it.' Valerie had long since given up any hope of getting him to budge on that.

He'd dreaded Dave asking him *'So what do you do for a living?'* Because Jim was an awful liar. The times he'd wished he could be more like Gary, his handsome gay detective, who could make angels weep when he spoke. *Gary* never got flustered or tongue-tied. Gary could look someone in the eye and lie convincingly.

Yeah, but Gary's not real, remember? And Gary is about to be killed off—metaphorically speaking. Him and Mick.

Jim was tired of them. He was tired of writing about this married pair who were as in love with each other now as the day they'd—fictionally—first met. He was tired of writing fade-to-black scenes, of closing the bedroom door. Gary and Mick didn't have sex because that would detract from the story, he told Valerie over and over again when she asked him to sex up the books. Jim didn't write erotic thrillers, he told her—he wrote detective stories where Gary and Mick always outwitted the bad guy(s), and where it didn't matter what they did behind closed doors—that was no one's business but theirs. And while that wasn't a lie, it wasn't the truth either.

Jim couldn't write about sex or love or affection. It would feel false. Sure, he could fake it. There were enough books containing gay sex scenes out there for him to get some inspiration, but that felt… wrong. And it all boiled down to one thing.

How in the hell can I write convincing sex scenes when I'm celibate?

Chapter 2

Julian Ingram stretched beneath the comforter as his husband Michael came into their bedroom carrying two mugs of hot chocolate. "I must've been really good in a previous life to deserve you," he murmured.

Michael merely chuckled as he deposited the mugs on the nightstand before climbing into bed. Julian snuggled up against him, until Michael's cold feet touched his. He shivered and Michael laughed. "Love me, love my cold feet."

Julian huffed. "You're lucky I love you. Anyone else, they'd be on the rug by now." He craned his neck to look at Michael. "Has it been a good day?"

"I think so." He put his arm around Julian, holding him close. "It's going to be beautiful when it's finished."

"How many more pieces will you need?" Julian asked. Michael had been hard at work all day in his studio, stopping to grab a bite at lunchtime. Julian had resorted to banging on the door at seven. He knew if he left Michael to his own devices, he'd work all the hours God sent. Not that Julian had seen Michael's present sculpture. That was only allowed when he was done.

Julian was the same with his paintings. Michael knew better than to cross the threshold of his studio.

"Maybe three more bears. You know they always sell. Then I'll have to think what else I'd like to do." Michael smiled. "I've got this gorgeous piece of wood.

It's crying out to be a nude."

Julian chuckled. "Which is what I'm working on at the moment." He had photos of their friends Ben and Anthony that he'd taken on their last visit in the summer. Julian had taken them into the woods, then persuaded them to disrobe. Not that they'd needed much persuasion. Julian had taken photos of the two of them against a tree trunk, Anthony behind Ben, his arms around him, Ben's head resting against Anthony's shoulder. They gave off such an air of peace, so clearly lost in each other, that Julian had forgotten himself for a moment. Sunlight filtered through the canopy of leaves, dancing on their bodies, covering them in dappled shadow.

His wall was covered with the photos, and a couple of them were pinned to the top of his easel. Julian estimated he was three-quarters of the way through, but he was already getting excited.

The piece was going to be the best thing he'd ever done.

Then he remembered. "Did the new guest arrive?"

"Yes. Dave checked him in this afternoon."

"And?" Julian asked pointedly.

Michael laughed again. "Apparently, we'd like him. And let's face it. Dave knows our tastes by now."

Julian laid his head on Michael's broad chest. "I suppose it's too much to hope he's gay."

Michael snorted. "Wow. You *really* want your Christmas present early this year, don't you?" He warmed his hand first on his mug, then slid it below the comforter, stroking Julian's chest.

"See? I knew there was a reason why I like you," Julian said with a happy sigh.

"Only 'like'?" Suddenly, gentle fingers became

teasing, and Julian wriggled as Michael tickled his belly.

"Hey, cut that out!" He glared at Michael. "I thought we'd outgrown that."

Michael's eyes gleamed. "You're never too old to be tickled. You just react slower." He stopped, however, and Julian resumed his snuggling.

"And there's nothing wrong with wanting a little fun. It's winter. We've gotta get our fun where we can find it."

"Oh, I don't mind having some fun," Michael remarked, "as long as you remember the rule."

Julian rolled his eyes. "This is because of Grant, isn't it? All we did was kiss." Christ, that was two months ago. Grant had been staying for a week, and oh my *God* was he cute. Better than cute—he was goddamn *perfect*. Lots of fur, a beard, and a belly that cried out for Julian to rest his head there. He'd come for cocktails his first evening, and had stayed for a whole lot more. "And I seem to recall *you* enjoying that furry ass of his several times during his stay." And *what* an ass. Julian could have rimmed that tight little hole till Rapture.

"Oh, he was a joy to fuck, no argument from me." Michael speared him with a hard stare. "My problem was, you were in his cabin when you first kissed him. Without me. And the only reason you got found out was because he'd left his phone on our coffee table, I went over to give it back, and walked in on you two making out." He sighed. "You *know* I have no objection to you kissing other guys—as long as I'm there." He lifted Julian's chin with two fingers, and looked him in the eye. "Humor me. What's the rule?"

Julian sighed. "We play together, and only if we're both attracted to the guy—or guys," he added with a smile. Not that the rule was a hardship. It had worked for them for the past twenty-five years. During that time, they'd seen a lot of their friends' relationships fall by the wayside, while theirs had stayed the course.

The rule works, no doubt about that. As for the longevity of their relationship, Julian put it down to three things—communication, expectations, and honesty. They were happy with each other, and what they had was strong. But occasionally gay men would come to stay at the cabins, and if there was a spark of something, Julian and Michael invited him—or them—to share their bed. It was fun and there were no strings, just men enjoying one another.

Then the guests would leave, and Julian and Michael returned to their happy life. They weren't forever waiting to see who turned up next. The occasional third—or couple—was just the icing on the cake now and then.

Yup. It works.

Michael's soft stroking over his belly and chest was certainly working. Not that Julian's dick needed much encouragement: the sight of Michael naked was enough.

That can't be bad, right? He's fifty-two, I'm fifty, we've been together a quarter of a century, and he still turns me on. Hell, Michael could do that with just a look. The one that said Get-your-ass-in-that-bedroom-because-I-need-to-be-inside-you-in-less-than-five-minutes.

Julian smiled. *As if it ever takes Michael that long when he's horny.* "Can you remember if there's ever been anyone we *weren't* both attracted to?"

Michael stroked his beard thoughtfully. "Now that you mention it…" He chuckled. "Okay. You got me."

"And you *know* I would have told you about kissing Grant, don't you?" There were no secrets. That was the unwritten rule, one Julian had never broken. Secrets spelled disaster for a relationship, because they always had a habit of surfacing, and never in a good way.

Michael kissed his forehead. "I know, babe." He paused. "Dave said he gets the feeling this one wants to be left to his own devices."

It took Julian a second or two to realize they were back to discussing their new guest. *You think I'd be used to the way his mind works by now.* Michael's butterfly brain flitted from one topic to another with little or no warning. "Ah, gotcha. So no slipping over there to invite him for a cocktail tomorrow night? Or mulled wine, which is probably a better idea, given the temperature."

"Better not. He made it clear he was here for the peace and solitude, so let's steer clear of him."

Something stirred at the back of Julian's mind. "Wait a minute. Is he the guest who negotiated a deal for a month's stay?" They'd never had anyone stay that long before.

"That's him. So he's going to be with us for Christmas too."

Julian blinked. "We're not going to leave him alone then, surely? Who *is* this guy, the Grinch?"

Michael laughed. "Oh dear Lord. I can hear your brain ticking over already." He cupped Julian's chin once more, and met his gaze. "Leave. Him. Alone. Got it?"

Julian sighed. "Got it." He rolled his eyes. "Spoilsport."

"*Someone* has to keep an eye on you." Then Michael smiled as a fuzzy shape landed on their bed with a soft *whump*. "Well, hello there, Buster Bear. You've decided to join us for the night?"

Their wiry little brown, grey-muzzled Patterdale crept up the bed, stepping over them until he reached their chests. Julian scritched behind Buster's ears. "Did you get lonely in your bed? Is that it?" Buster flopped onto Michael's chest, butting his head under Michael's chin, and Julian chuckled. "Don't get too comfy, Buster. You're not gonna want to stay there long."

"Why not?" Michael asked with a frown. Then he grinned. "You have plans, don't you?"

Julian said nothing, but leaned across and kissed him, drinking in his husband's familiar scent, loving the soft scratch of Michael's beard against his cheek. Then he gave a leisurely roll until he was lying face down, his hips tilted in invitation.

He caught Michael's chuckle. "Oh, I see. You *definitely* have plans." Julian heard the soft thud of four paws on the rug. "Sorry, Buster." Not that Buster would've stayed anyway. He'd be back when the loving was done. Then Michael's weight was on Julian, his lips pressed to Julian's shoulders in the gentlest of kisses. "You need me?" he whispered.

Julian turned his head to meet the kiss he knew awaited him. "Always," he whispered back before Michael claimed his lips, taking his time.

Michael's breath tickled his ear. "Tell me what you want."

Fuck. Julian loved their ritual exchanges that always preceded lovemaking. He shivered. "I want you inside me."

"Where I belong?" Michael released his mouth and kissed a path down his spine.

"Where you belong," Julian vowed. He shuddered as Michael tugged his hips higher before pulling his cheeks apart. He blew gently on Julian's hole, sending ripples of anticipation through him. Julian spread his knees as wide as he could, inviting Michael in, and that first touch of Michael's tongue pushed a low groan from him, as it always did.

Julian propped himself up on his elbows, staring at the mirror on the wall above their pillows. He caught his breath at the sight of Michael burying his face in Julian's crack, his dick rock-hard at the sound of Michael's appreciative noises as he dove deep. Michael's gaze met his, his eyes locked on Julian's as he rimmed him, his fingers digging into the firm flesh of his ass. Julian rocked his hips, loving the slip and slide of Michael's tongue over his hole.

Then it was over, and Michael was crawling up Julian's body, his gaze still focused on Julian's reflection. "Ready for me?" Michael's heavy cock slid between his ass cheeks, moving over his hole in a tantalizingly slow dance.

"Tease." Julian reached for the lube and passed it back to him. He held his breath, awaiting that first breach, the one that always made him shudder with sensual delight. Michael guided his dick into position, then his lips ghosted down the back of Julian's neck as he entered him, slow as you please, as though they had all the time in the world.

Julian let out a sigh of pleasure as Michael filled him to the hilt. "Welcome home," he whispered.

Michael put his weight on his hands and began that delicious slow in-and-out, their eyes locked on the reflection as he made love to Julian, the air filled with soft sighs and murmured words of love. The rhythmic movement of Michael's ass as he rocked into him was mesmerizing, the slow roll of his hips as he filled Julian again and again. Julian lost himself in the sensuous rhythm, enjoying the hitch in Michael's breathing when Julian tightened his muscles around the thick shaft that stretched him so gloriously.

"Soon, babe," Michael whispered.

Julian nodded, aware of the slight quickening of Michael's thrusts. Julian rocked with him, pushing up to meet his dick. When Michael came, it was with a sigh as he filled Julian, his arms tight around Julian's shoulders, anchoring himself.

When Michael was once more at peace, he eased out of Julian, then rolled him onto his back. Julian gave a low cry as Michael took his cock deep, and it wasn't long before he pulsed into Michael's waiting mouth. Julian shuddered as Michael cleaned him with his tongue, then stretched out beside him.

"Was that what you needed?" Michael kissed Julian's damp chest.

"You know it." Julian glanced at the mugs. "So much for the hot chocolate."

"I can heat it up while you clean up." Michael kissed his forehead before getting out of bed and heading for the kitchen. By the time Julian exited the bathroom, Michael was already waiting for him. Julian got into bed and held out his hand for his mug.

"What do we know about this guest?" Julian was trying to appear nonchalant, but his interest was piqued.

"Not much. He didn't fill in the further information box when he reserved the cabin, I know that much." Michael gave Julian a stern glance. "Do I have to repeat myself? Leave him alone."

Julian let out an exaggerated sigh. "Sure." He sipped his chocolate, going over all the ways he could *accidentally* drop in on their mystery guest.

He'd think of something, that was for sure.

Chapter 3

When the sun rose, Jim rose with it. Period.

It was one of the routines that worked for him, and he saw no reason to change it. Besides, dawn in the middle of a forest was nothing like dawn in San Francisco. The sense of peace was awe-inspiring, and he stood on the balcony, a mug of coffee in his hand, sipping the freshly brewed nectar and drinking in the near silence.

It wasn't long, however, before he felt the tug of the laptop.

He had work to do. He had a book to finish.

Jim knew from his notes he was five chapters or so from the end. Five more chapters, and *au revoir*, Gary and Mick Buchanan. *Or should that be adieu?* He was torn between regret and anticipation. The fictional detectives had been part of his life for ten years, after all. He knew every facet of their lives, all of it written down in his bible, a sturdy notebook where he kept his notes about them. The only thing he hadn't decided upon was the final chapter—their exit. That part still eluded him. It had crossed his mind several times that the reason for this was that deep down, he really didn't want to let them go.

Jim was trying to ignore that feeling.

Work would begin after breakfast, and he was more than ready for it. Jim set the pan on the stove and grabbed the bacon from the refrigerator. It wasn't long before the delicious aroma filled the small cabin, and Jim's mouth watered. The eggs were already beaten, ready to go into the pan once the bacon was ready.

The bacon was almost done when a faint whimper caught his ears. Jim stilled, listening intently. There it was again, accompanied this time by a scratching sound.

Oh my God. There's a bear outside, trying to get into the cabin.

Then he reconsidered. He couldn't claim to be a bear expert, but to his knowledge, bears didn't whimper. When another whimper came, louder this time, followed by more soft scratches, Jim summoned up all his courage and went to the door. He had to know. He unlocked it, turned the handle, and opened it up just a crack so he could peer outside.

Nothing.

Then the whimper came again, and he glanced down. A small brown dog sat on the mat, gazing expectantly at him.

Jim opened the door, and the dog trotted into the cabin, headed straight for the stove, and then sat in front of it, licking its chops.

Jim couldn't help but smile. "Well, good morning."

The dog wagged its tail.

That was all the invitation Jim required. He went over to the stove and crouched down, stroking the wiry animal down its back. "Hello there. You got a name?" There was a collar, but he didn't have chance to look for a tag before the dog put its paws on Jim's knee and stretched up toward him.

Jim laughed. "Now, are you trying to give me a good morning lick, or are you trying to get closer to the bacon?" His money was on the latter, although there was no denying the dog was a friendly little thing. Not so young, either, judging by the amount of gray in its muzzle.

"Buster!"

Jim stiffened at the cry from outside. The dog's ears pricked up too. "Sounds like someone is looking for you." He peered at the dog. "Is that your name? Buster?"

The dog's ears twitched, and that tail picked up speed.

He laughed again. "Hello there, Buster. Pleased to make your acquaintance."

"Buster!" The voice was nearer.

Jim sighed. *Looks like I'm about to have company.* Thank God he'd gotten dressed. He rose to his feet and stared at the dog. "I think I'm safe to go to the door. There's no way you can reach the stove." He went over to the cabin door and called out, "Hello? I think what you're looking for—or rather, *who*—is in here."

A minute later, a tall, gray-haired man was climbing the steps to the cabin door. He wore a thick jacket and red scarf, and in his hand was a leash. Jim recognized him from the online photo—this was one of the owners.

The man gave him an apologetic look. "I'm so sorry. Is Buster being a nuisance?"

Jim chuckled. "Buster is just being a dog. I think the smell of the bacon lured him here." He froze. "Oh Lord, the bacon." He dashed back into the cabin, in time to see smoke rising from the pan. "Aw, crap." Jim hurried over to the stove and turned off heat.

The bacon was well and truly cremated.

The man came into the kitchen area and frowned at Buster. "You distracted him, didn't you?" Buster was at the guy's feet in an instant, stretching up, his front paws on the man's knees, tail wagging. The man scooped him into his arms, and got a doggy kiss.

The first thought to cross Jim's mind was that at least he wasn't the only one who spoke to dogs as if they were people. The second was that his host was a good-looking man. But before he could utter a word, the man held out a hand, the other supporting Buster.

"Hi. I'm Michael Ingram."

Jim shook. "You're one of the owners."

Michael blinked. "Yes." Then he smiled. "Ah. The photo on the website. And you're Jim Traynor. Who has the distinction of being the only guest to book such a long stay." He glanced at the pan, then met Jim's gaze. "I am so sorry. Allow me to offer you breakfast to make up for Buster's untimely intrusion."

For a moment Jim was stunned into silence. He cleared his throat. "That's okay. You don't need to do that."

"But I do. If Buster hadn't distracted you…"

Jim held up his hand. "It's okay, really. I have other things I can eat." The eggs, for one thing. "Besides, I'll be starting work as soon as I've eaten. That's me, a creature of habit." And being a creature of habit meant he didn't want his routine disturbed.

Michael frowned. "You're working? On a Sunday?"

Jim snorted. "I don't know about other writers, but I don't think like that. When there's a book to be finished, every day is a workday."

Shit. Here it comes. You're a writer? Wow. What do you write? Would I have heard of you? He steeled himself for the barrage of intrusive questions. *I should've kept my stupid mouth shut.*

"Well, assuming you're not going to be working until midnight… Can I at least invite you to join me and my husband for a cocktail this evening?" Michael smiled again. "We're creatures of habit too. Every night it's cocktails at seven. You'd be welcome to join us. It's the least I can do to make up for you losing out on your bacon."

"I do have more bacon, you know." That came out harsher than Jim had intended, and he sighed. "I'm sorry. It's just that I have my day planned."

Michael nodded. "I understand. Buster and I will get out of your hair." He turned and headed for the door, Jim following, with the intention of locking it as soon as they were out of sight. Michael paused at the threshold. "But in case you change your mind… remember the entrance to the site? Well, on the right was a lane. That leads to our house. You can't miss us. It's the only property." One last smile. "And now I really will leave you alone. My apologies for having disturbed your morning." He gave another glance in the direction of the kitchen area, his eyes twinkling. "Look on the bright side. Now you have bacon bits for a salad, if you need them."

And with that, he and Buster were gone.

Jim drew in a long, deep breath. He wouldn't have struck up such a conversation in normal circumstances—that had been down to Buster. And he genuinely hadn't minded the cute little dog who scratched at his door. Michael's invitations to both breakfast and a drink had surprised him, and he got the feeling Michael was a good guy.

Not that Jim had any intention of getting to know him further.

He gazed at the crispy bacon, and he had to smile. *Bacon bits*. That told him one thing—Michael had a sense of humor. Then he scraped the contents of the pan into the trash, and got on with cooking more.

Never mind the cute little dog and its sexy owner—I have work to do.

It wasn't until the second lot of bacon was sizzling that the thought sank in. Michael was sexy, there was no disputing that.

What surprised the hell out of Jim was that he'd *noticed.*

Julian wiped his brush on a rag as he stepped back from the canvas. He'd been working on the flesh tones, and they weren't quite right.

That usually meant it was time to take a break and come back to it with fresh eyes. He could afford a break—he'd been working since dawn because he loved the early morning light—and it was time for breakfast anyhow.

Michael's soft knock at the door took him by surprise.

"You can come in."

Michael stuck his head around the door. "Are you sure?"

Julian laughed. "Relax. Your timing is impeccable."

Michael came into the studio, not gazing at the canvas. He knew better. Not that Julian was such a diva that he wouldn't allow his husband to look at his work, but they had a routine. When Julian got to the stage where he had the feeling he was fiddling with it, that was when Michael was given permission to step in to tell him to stop, or to point out what needed doing.

"Just thought I'd let you know." Michael smiled. "I just met our new guest." Buster was in his arms, his head tucked under Michael's chin as always.

Julian's jaw dropped, and he gave Michael a hard stare. "Hey, no fair. *You* said we were to leave him alone." He mimicked Michael's voice. "'Do I have to repeat myself? Leave him alone.'"

Michael folded his arms. "Don't you use that schoolteacher voice with me. And I didn't go there deliberately. Buster followed his nose. The guy was cooking." Buster's ears pricked up at the sound of his name.

Julian walked over to them and scritched Buster behind his ears. "Buster, you good dog."

Michael narrowed his gaze. "You... you couldn't have trained him to do that, could you?"

Julian gaped. "As if I'd do a thing like that." Buster got another scritch. "What can I say? Like Daddy, like son."

"He was cooking bacon at the time."

Julian rolled his eyes. "Well, that explains it. Our little bacon lover here would have been over there in a heartbeat." He put down his rag and brush, and placed his hands on his hips. "Well?"

Michael gazed back at him with an innocent expression. "Well, what?"

Julian narrowed his gaze. "You know full well what I want to know. What's he like?"

Michael gave a shrug. "He seems okay. A bit of a workaholic, if you ask me. Buster distracted him from his cooking, so I offered to make him breakfast when the bacon ended up cremated."

Julian blinked. "Did he say yes?" He assessed how quickly he could shower.

"Before you start making plans, he said no. He has work to do."

He glared at Michael. "You could've invited him for a cocktail tonight."

Michael's lips twitched. "I did. But I get the feeling he's not interested.

"He's got work? What does he do?" Julian's interest was piqued.

"He's a writer, he said."

"And? What does he write?" Christ, it was like getting blood from a stone. Then he reasoned Michael was being deliberately obtuse because he knew he could.

"I don't know, he didn't tell me, and I didn't ask."

"Why on earth not?"

It was Michael's turn to give a hard stare. "Because that would have been nosy, and we already know he wants to be left alone. Don't we?" he added in a meaningful tone. "And before you get all excited, don't. He's not going to show tonight."

"How do you know?" Not that Julian doubted Michael's instincts. They were usually on-the-nail.

Another shrug. "Just what my gut's telling me." He peered at Julian. "Now, are you ready to eat, or do you want to go back to work?"

"Eat. I need a break anyhow." He dipped his brush into the turps and cleaned it before wiping it again. As they walked out of the studio, Michael leaned in and kissed him on the neck.

"So, am I forgiven?"

"For what?"

Michael grinned. "Getting the first glimpse of our

enigmatic guest."

"I suppose so." Julian feigned reluctant acceptance.

"By the way…" Another gentle kiss. "David was right."

He came to a halt. "What?"

That got him another grin. "You'd *really* like him."

Julian was about to glare, when Michael's words hit home. "Aha!" he declared triumphantly. "That means *you* like him too." Which only firmed his resolve to meet this guy, one way or another.

Chapter 4

Getting away from San Francisco had to be the best decision ever.

It had taken him four days, but the book was finally finished. And as always, he couldn't wait to send it on its way. He'd managed to text Valerie the previous day—when he'd gotten a signal—so she knew it was coming. Now all he had to do was submit it.

Except there was no Wi-Fi.

Nothing.

Nada.

Zilch.

Jim was tearing his hair out.

The book was already overdue, for Christ's sake, thanks to freaking writer's block. When he'd sat down to write on Sunday morning, there had been that brief stab of fear when the blank page stared back at him, as it had done so often in recent months. He had his notes. He knew what was supposed to happen. It was simply a matter of putting it into some cohesive order. What eluded him was the dialogue. It just wasn't coming. But then he'd heard a snatch of banter in his head, and he'd scrambled to commit it to the page.

The dam burst, the proverbial floodgates opened, and a torrent of words gushed through.

Thank God.

Except what did that matter when he couldn't submit the goddamn book?

He'd tried disconnecting and reconnecting to the internet. Nothing. In desperation, he grabbed the folder and searched for Dave's number. All he got was his voicemail.

Dave was not available.

Jim knew he wouldn't be able to relax until he'd sent the book on its way. *And if Mohammed won't come to the mountain…* That left one option—to go find the mountain himself.

The owners will know what to do, right? Hell, they might even have Wi-Fi.

In his frazzled state, Jim was willing to do just about anything for a little peace.

He tucked his laptop into its bag, put on his thick coat and scarf, squeezed his feet into his boots—hell, he'd worn nothing but winter socks since he'd arrived six days ago—and headed for the door.

There was little snow on the path that led through the site, and Jim figured someone had been out clearing it at some point. He walked briskly through the forest, following the exit signs dotted here and there. He reckoned it was a ten-minute stroll to the site entrance. Once he'd reached it, he peered down the lane, but there was no sign of a house. But as it was the only lane in evidence, it had to be the right one.

Jim headed up the narrow road, surrounded by trees on both sides. The sunlight managed to break here and there, and where it hit, the snow had melted. After a few minutes, he finally caught sight of a rooftop and headed for it.

When he stepped into the small clearing, Jim was stunned into silence. The house was a beautiful mix of timber and glass, with much of the front given over to windows. Inside, he glimpsed a high ceiling, and what appeared to be a mezzanine. The snow had been cleared around the house and in the driveway. The property looked at one with its surroundings, nestled amongst the trees.

The kind of place Jim felt he could happily live in.

He couldn't see a front door, so he strolled around to the side and found a porch. Through the glass door, he spied a familiar figure, and he crouched down.

"Well, hello again, Buster."

The friendly little dog came up to the glass and put his front paws up on it, his tail wagging.

"Is your daddy home? Well, at least one of your daddies?" Jim smiled to himself. *If Buster answered, I'd shit a brick.* Of course, ringing the doorbell might have been a good way to find out. But when no one appeared, he figured he was screwed—until he caught the faint sound of classical music. It was coming from the nearest of two outbuildings that stood farther back from the house. They were of a similar size, roughly that of a double garage, both with gables, and the front was taken up with windows that reached the peak of the roof. Paths had been cleared from the house to both buildings.

Someone's obviously home.

Jim wasn't ready to give up just yet.

Peeking in through the window felt wrong, so he went over to the building and knocked on the side door. "Hello?"

"Who is it?"

Jim didn't think that was Michael's voice. "It's Jim Traynor. I'm staying in one of your cabins, and I've got a problem."

"Have you tried to contact Dave?"

The person speaking didn't sound irate, but Jim got

the sense he was intruding. *This was a bad idea.* He'd get in his car, drive to the nearest town, and find a Starbucks or someplace with Wi-Fi.

"Look, it's okay. I'll sort it out myself. Sorry to have bothered you." He walked away, but seconds later he heard the door open.

"Wait."

Jim turned. This was Julian Ingram, and judging by his appearance, he was a painter. He wore a white lab coat over his clothes, which was smeared with different colors, and in one hand he held a rag.

"You haven't bothered me," Julian said. "I wasn't expecting anyone. I take it Dave's not available?"

"That's right. You were my last hope," he said with a smile.

Julian bit his lip. "Well, far be it from me to dash that hope. What's the problem?"

Without going into any details as to why he needed Wi-Fi so urgently, Jim explained the situation.

Julian nodded. "Yeah, the router can be a little temperamental. I'll come back with you, and sort it out. Plus, I'll show you what to do if it does it again."

"Oh no, please. You're working."

Julian's smile seemed genuine. "And it's time I took a break anyway. Besides, Buster could do with a walk. He's been cooped up in the house all day. Just let me leave a note for Michael, in case he comes looking. Not that *that's* likely." He inclined his head toward the farthest outbuilding. "He's been at it since dawn." Julian went back inside, and returned a minute later with a Post-it that he stuck to the door. He stared at it for a minute, then went back inside, returning with a piece of tape, with which he secured the Post-it. Julian gave him a grin. "They're notoriously bad at staying stuck to anything. Now, let me go and get my jacket. Buster will be so excited." He grinned. "You've met him, haven't you? Michael said the smell of your bacon was too much for Buster to resist." He beckoned with his hand. "Come and wait in the warm."

Jim followed him into the house, and the change in temperature was delightful. He waited by the door as a very enthusiastic Buster greeted Julian, stretching up for cuddles. Jim might not have been a great fan of people, but animals were something else, and he trusted their judgment.

"I won't be a sec," Julian told him. "I just have to use the bathroom." He left Jim by the door, Buster trotting behind him.

Apparently, Buster needed to use the bathroom too.

Jim glanced at his surroundings. The windows and high ceiling gave the room a light, airy feel, and the thick rugs on the hardwood floor added to the impression. He peered up at the mezzanine with its wooden railings, wondering if the bedrooms were there.

Below, three sofas made a U-shape, placed around a log burner, and Jim was surprised not to see a TV screen in evidence. A square Chinese rug filled the space between the sofas, and small wooden tables sat at each corner. The walls were covered with paintings, and he wondered if these were Julian's work. Jim couldn't resist wandering over to take a closer look at the large canvas that covered most of the chimney breast above the log burner.

It was a portrait of Michael, sitting on a large boulder in a clearing in the middle of a forest, and he was nude. Judging by the color of his hair, and the silvery hairs on his chest, it was a fairly recent painting.

What impressed Jim most was the feeling of peace the painting imbued. The light was incredible, giving his skin a warm glow.

"I did that last year."

Jim gave a start. Julian joined him, dressed in a thick jacket and scarf. He stood next to Jim, gazing up at the portrait.

"You're very talented." He gestured to the walls. "Are these all yours?"

Julian nodded. "Some of them are from when I first started painting, almost thirty years ago." He smiled. "I've learned a lot." Julian inclined his head toward the door. "Let's go sort out your Wi-Fi."

Jim followed him out of the house and along the lane, Buster trotting in front of them on his leash, sniffing at grass or inspecting tree trunks. When he began to tug, Julian laughed. "Okay then." He bent down and unclipped the leash, and Buster was off in a heartbeat, sprinting ahead of them before running back to circle Julian, then doing it all over again.

Jim smiled. "He reminds me of a poster I saw once. It was a puppy bounding along, with the slogan, 'Live life like someone left the gate open.'"

Julian chuckled. "As far as Buster is concerned, he's still a puppy, even if he's twelve." He glanced at Jim. "Michael tells me you're a writer."

"Yes." Jim steeled himself for the questions.

Julian said nothing, but bent down to pick up a chunky stick. "Hey, Buster. Look what I've found."

Buster stilled in the middle of the lane, took one look at Julian, and pelted toward him, tail wagging. Julian launched the stick into the air, and Buster chased it.

"He still moves like a puppy," Jim commented.

"And as long as we keep giving him supplements for his hips and joints, it'll stay that way." Julian waited as Buster ran back to him, the stick carried proudly in his mouth. "Good boy."

Jim swore Buster was going to wag that tail right off.

Julian threw it again, and they continued walking. "Is everything okay with the cabin? Apart from the Wi-Fi, of course."

"Everything's fine," Jim assured him. "The peace and quiet is exactly what I needed."

"We love it here." Julian's voice was quiet. "We don't miss the noise, the dirt, and the congestion of the big cities, not one bit. Life here is just perfect."

"Does all this inspire you?" Jim gestured to the trees surrounding them.

Julian nodded. "It's hard not to be inspired when you're surrounded by so much beauty." He smiled. "Who knows what it will inspire *you* to write?"

Jim was hoping for exactly that. He had no idea what lay around the corner, now that he'd finally finished the series. It was a little scary, if he were honest.

"If you want to see what else this area has to offer, we'd be pleased to show you around." Julian grinned. "We have to take a day off occasionally."

It was a kind offer, but Jim didn't think he'd be taking Julian up on it anytime soon. "I wouldn't want to impose."

Julian waved his hand. "No imposition, I assure you." He gave Jim another glance. "Maybe some inspiration is what you need."

For the first time in a long while, Jim felt *seen*, and he didn't know how to react.

They fell into a comfortable silence, accompanied by the sounds of birds chirping, and the rustle of the trees in the slight breeze. Jim took the opportunity to get a better look at his host. Julian was shorter than Michael, with short gray hair and a neat beard and mustache. Where Michael's eyes were blue, his were brown. The way he filled his jacket spoke of time spent lifting weights, and overall he gave an impression of solidity and calm self-assurance.

Jim had to admit both men were handsome.

They reached Jim's cabin, and instead of climbing the wooden steps that led to the door, Julian went beneath it to another door, obviously a basement of some kind. He led Jim inside, Buster following them, sniffing the board-covered floor. There wasn't much to be seen, only a pair of step ladders, cleaning supplies, and a couple of chairs.

"This isn't kept locked." Julian pointed to a shelf where the router sat. "Now, if this happens again, remove this cable… then this one…. then plug them in again and press this button here on top of the router. Wait a minute, then try the Wi-Fi." He sighed. "It can be a little temperamental. You just have to know how to treat it."

Jim got out his phone and glanced at it. "Hey," he said with a smile.

Julian chuckled. "Success, I take it." He led the way out of the space, and closed the door. "Now you know what to do next time it happens. And there *will* be a next time."

"Thank you," Jim said earnestly. "I'm sorry to have taken you away from your painting."

That got him another wave. "It was fine. Like I said, I was due for a break. Plus, it gave Buster an opportunity to chase sticks."

At the word sticks, Buster's ears pricked up.

Julian laughed. "Okay, we'll go find some more." He addressed Jim. "I know Michael has already invited you for a drink, but I'm extending the invitation again. We'd be happy for you to join us. Now you know the way." His eyes twinkled.

Before Jim could respond with a polite refusal, Julian clicked his fingers. "Come on, Buster. Let's leave Jim to his work." They walked away from the cabin, Buster running ahead making a happy yipping sound.

Jim watched until they were out of sight, then hurried indoors to open the laptop and send the manuscript. The Wi-Fi connected, he attached the file, and like that, his precious final book was gone, into the ether.

Jim was accustomed to the writer-drop that accompanied every submission. It was always such an anticlimax, and for a moment he felt at a loss as for what to do next. Edits would follow, he knew that, because Valerie never wasted time forwarding his manuscripts, especially as the publisher was waiting on this one.

Would it be so bad to have a drink with them this evening?

It wasn't as if he had anything better to do. In fact, if it meant he didn't have to think about his next, so far non-existent project, so much the better. Jim could afford to break his routine, and the couple seemed friendly and amusing. Besides, he wanted to know what Michael did in that outbuilding.

That did it. Jim was having a cocktail that evening.

Michael had to smile when he caught Julian gazing at the clock for the fifth time that evening. "He's not coming," he said gently.

Julian turned to fire something at him, but his eyes sparkled as he glanced toward the window. "Then who's that walking up to our door?"

Michael froze. "Seriously?" It was almost a week since Jim had arrived, and Michael had given up hope of him turning up at the house. He hurried to the door. Jim stood there, bundled up against the cold night air.

Michael opened it. "Get in, it's freezing out there." He waited while Jim removed his jacket, scarf and gloves, and then hung them on a hook, placing the gloves on the table. "You can leave your boots on the mat. Then come on in and get warm." He left Jim to remove his boots, and walked into the living area.

Julian stood by the drinks cabinet, wearing a smug grin. *See?* he mouthed.

Jim stepped into the room, and Julian greeted him with a wide smile. "Hey, you made it. Take a seat by the fire, and I'll get you a drink." He chuckled as Buster got up from his dog bed and trotted over to Jim. "Your cocktail comes with Buster, because he *will* jump on your lap. Just put him down if that's not okay."

Jim sat on the sofa, and Buster leapt into his lap. "It's fine." He stroked Buster's head, and Buster got comfortable.

Michael laughed. "You *were* going to stay there all

night, weren't you? Now, what are you drinking? Julian makes for a great bartender, and we're well stocked with alcohol."

Julian snorted. "*Now* you see why he married me, for my bartending skills."

"Could I have a margarita?"

Michael beamed. "Great choice. Bested only by his Mai Tai, which is phenomenal." Julian got to it, and Michael sat facing Jim. "So, was everything okay once you got the Wi-Fi working?"

Jim nodded. "I had to submit a manuscript. All done."

Michael couldn't contain his curiosity a moment longer. "Look, I don't mean to pry, but… what do you write?"

"Books," Jim replied promptly in a deadpan voice.

Julian chuckled. "Nice one. Is this going to turn out to be twenty questions, or is what you write a secret?"

Jim appeared to deliberate for a moment. "I write murder mysteries."

Michael caught his breath, and Julian laughed. "Oh, you've done it now. You've only gone and named his favorite genre."

"Have you been writing long?" Michael asked.

Jim gave a shrug. "About ten years."

"Do you write about a particular sleuth?" Michael wanted to know if Jim's books were on his shelf. When he'd told Julian about Jim's profession, Julian had Googled him and found nothing. Michael had snorted before asking if Julian had ever heard of the concept of a pseudonym.

"A pair of sleuths, actually. They're a married couple, called Gary and Mick Buchanan."

Oh my God. Michael had chills. "You're… you're Dayton O'Connell."

Jim blinked. "Well, yes."

Michael pointed to his bookshelf. "I have all your books."

Julian laughed. "This, Jim, is the moment where you run, before he turns all Kathy Bates on you, and tells you he's your number one fan." His eyes widened. "Oh my God. A snowy landscape. A remote setting." His eyes sparkled. "Don't look now, Jim, but you've wandered onto the set for *Misery*." He glanced at Michael with a wicked glint in his eye. "If he brings out a mallet and a block of wood, I'd start running. While you still can."

To Michael's delight, Jim burst out laughing. "I think we're safe. I don't recall there being a dog in *Misery*. And Buster will save me, won't you, Buster?"

At the sound of his name, Buster raised his head, then settled back down.

Julian cackled. "Only if there are treats involved." Buster's ears pricked up at that, and Julian groaned. "Dammit. I said the T-word." He grabbed a fat jar from a shelf, opened it, and removed a bone-shaped cookie. Buster crunched it up in seconds.

Michael had about a million questions, but he reasoned this was not the time, not if he wanted Jim to come back another evening. "Would you come for a drink tomorrow night? I'd love to talk to you about your books. I love them. I've been a fan since the first one."

Jim flushed. "Believe it or not, I'm not used to this. I'm a little… overwhelmed."

Michael could understand that. He knew from his research that Dayton O'Connell didn't do public appearances or social media. And after meeting Jim, he could understand why. *Maybe he's not a people person.* But he wrote amazing books.

"You'd be welcome to come have a drink with us every night of your stay," Julian said. "Believe me, it would take that long for Michael to get out all his questions and stop fangirling you."

Michael gave him a mock glare. "I am *not* fangirling."

Julian rolled his eyes. "Oh, puh-*lease*. I'm expecting puppy dog eyes any second now. I bet you're itching to get Jim to sign every copy you possess, am I right?" He grinned. "Then it'll be the selfies."

Michael turned to Jim. "Don't listen. I have no such intentions. And Julian has no room to talk. He's done *his* share of fangirling, trust me."

Jim looked from Michael to Julian, and back to Michael again, then burst into laughter once more. "You two must have been together a while."

Michael chuckled. "It shows, huh?"

They spent the next half hour discussing Jim's first book, and Michael was pleased to see him relax a little. When he'd finished his second margarita, Jim sighed. "It's time I was out of here. I have to wake up early in the morning."

"A new book for Gary and Mick?" Michael asked, unable to repress his eagerness.

Jim bit his lip. "You know, Julian was closer with his *Misery* wisecracks than he could know. How about I tell you why tomorrow night?"

Michael smiled. "Then you'll come back?"

Jim nodded. "Yeah. I've really enjoyed tonight. Good company, great cocktails, and a heated cushion for my lap." He scritched behind Buster's ears before gently easing him onto the sofa beside him. Jim gave Julian a nod. "Thank you again for the invite."

"You're welcome." Julian rose to his feet, and they walked with Jim to the door. He bade them goodnight, and stepped out into night air.

Michael watched him through the window. *Well, I didn't expect that.* He was delighted Jim had dropped by, and the promise of more conversations to come sent a trickle of anticipation through him.

Julian joined him. "He's not gay."

Michael blinked. "He writes about two gay detectives. Did you miss that part?"

"Which he probably writes because writing LGBT characters is trending right now."

Michael stared at him. "Characters that he's been writing about for *ten years*. That doesn't seem like a trend to me."

"Well, tell me about these books of his. What are they like? Are they sexy? Do I need to read 'em?" Their taste in books was one of the few areas where they didn't match.

Michael chuckled. "There's no sex. Gary and Mick are an affectionate couple, but it's pretty much fade to black every time there's a hint of more."

Julian stared back at him. "See? He's not gay. If he were gay, he'd write them fucking like bunnies."

Michael bit back a smile. "I have one word to say to you—Marco."

Julian glared. "Oh, come *on*."

"Come on nothing. He was here for a week. I kept telling you I thought he was gay, but you? '*Noooo*, he's not gay'…" Michael grinned. "How many times did we fuck the last night of his stay? So forgive me if I don't pay any attention to your pronouncements. Your gaydar is not working."

Julian gave him a sideways glance. "But what do *you* think of Jim?"

That was easy. "I like him." He liked the whole package—brown hair, short enough on top to be a little spiky; a full beard and mustache; warm brown eyes, and that smile.... It had taken a while to get Jim to *reveal* that smile, but it was certainly worth it.

Julian's eyes held a familiar twinkle. "Me too."

Michael knew that expression. Julian's interest had definitely been piqued. And he wasn't alone. Julian's gaydar might've been faulty, but Michael trusted his own.

Chapter 5

When Friday morning came, it brought with it a heap of doubts. That was nothing new in itself. Jim was used to the onslaught that always followed the submission of a book. What *was* new was the feeling he'd made a mistake.

Should I have ended the series? Or do I write another?

The latter would mean changing the ending, and that wouldn't be a small task. As it was, he'd left no room for coming back to the series in the future, and maybe that *was* a mistake. Jim was in virgin territory, and it scared him to death. The prospect of dipping his toes—or should that be fingers?—into a completely new world left him unsettled and antsy.

More than that—he felt lost.

He sat on the balcony, his first cup of coffee clasped in his hands, staring out at the beautiful landscape that surrounded him. Changing the ending wasn't an option, he knew that. But maybe rewriting part of it, to allow for further development, could be possible.

No. No. You wanted it this way, remember? Besides, he had had enough of Gary and Mick and their perfect relationship. No couple could be that perfect, right? Except Jim knew why he'd written them that way. He'd created a couple whose relationship was nothing like the ones he saw around him. In essence, he'd written them how *he* wanted a relationship to be. And guys just weren't like that.

What about Julian and Michael?

Jim recalled their banter from the previous evening, the affection they plainly bore each other. He liked the way they were together, the love they shared. Only now he realized something. Julian and Michael were closer to his ideal fictional couple than anyone he'd met. They could *be* Gary and Mick.

You don't know that. You don't know them, not really.

But he wanted to. The idea of sitting alone in his cabin, waiting for inspiration to strike, had suddenly lost its appeal. He wanted company—*their* company.

On impulse, he pulled on his boots, put on his jacket and scarf, and left the cabin. The crisp morning air was invigorating as he strolled through the forest. Little sound penetrated it, apart from the chirp of birds and the rustle of the trees in the wind. He could have been the only person alive for miles.

Except for the little dog running toward him.

"Buster!" Jim smiled and crouched down to greet his new friend. Buster had his paws on Jim's knees in a heartbeat, and licked his face eagerly. Jim laughed. "I'm pleased to see you too."

"Buster Bear Ingram." Michael came into view, the leash in his hand. Buster left Jim and ran to him, circling him.

"Good morning." Jim rose to his feet. "No bacon this time, so I'm assuming he just wanted to say hi." At that moment his stomach growled, and he cursed silently.

Michael didn't react, however. "I think you've found a new friend."

Buster was back at Jim's feet, and he bent low to scritch him behind the ears. "He's welcome any time."

"I hope we're not disturbing you."

Jim shook his head. "You've caught me on the horns of a dilemma."

"Sounds painful." Michael cocked his head to one side. "Have you had breakfast yet?"

Jim bit his lip. "I rather think that thunder rumbling in my stomach tells you the answer to that question."

"Well, why not come back with me and Buster? Julian is making breakfast, and there'll be plenty for all of us, trust me." Michael's gaze met his. "Please, don't say no. We'd love to have you eat with us."

Jim didn't hesitate. "I'd love to. If you're sure it's no bother." It wasn't as if he had anything to work on, right? And he'd genuinely liked being around the couple.

Michael beamed. "No bother at all." He peered at Buster. "You hear that, Buster? Your new friend is coming home with us."

Buster was too busy sniffing the ground.

Jim laughed. "Whatever he's smelling is much more interesting than me."

They followed the path to the lane, Buster running for the sticks Michael threw for him. When they reached the house, Jim sighed. "I love your place. It looks like it was meant to be here."

Michael gave him a warm smile. "That's how we see it too." He led Jim around to the side porch, and pushed the door open. "Julian? We have a guest for breakfast."

"Oh?" Julian came into view, and Jim had to laugh at the sight of the apron that covered him. It depicted a naked man, with a six pack and a very long dick.

"You'll have to excuse my husband's taste,"

Michael said quickly. "What makes it worse is he designed it, then a friend made it for him."

"There's nothing wrong with my taste," Julian declared with an indignant air. "You only have to look at Michael to know that." His eyes sparkled. He gave Jim a welcoming smile. "Hello again. Take off your jacket and boots, then come in. I'll put more bacon on." Then he disappeared back into the kitchen.

Jim did as instructed, leaving his boots on the mat by the door. Michael led him into the kitchen, which was large with a high ceiling, the rear wall comprising nothing but windows that looked out over the back yard. He could see the two outbuildings, and the sight stirred his curiosity.

"What do you do, Michael? For a living, I mean."

Before Michael could respond, Julian said, "He's a sculptor and wood carver."

Jim blinked. "You're both creative people."

Michael gazed at him with obvious interest. "That seems to surprise you."

He shrugged. "I'd have thought that having two people with an artistic temperament in such close proximity would lead to frequent conflicts, but you seem so…"

"Happy? Relaxed?" Michael grinned. "You thought we'd be at each other's throats?"

Julian chuckled. "You should have seen us when we were in our twenties. A very different story. What you see now is the result of years of patience, compromise, and routine. I stay out of his space, he stays out of mine."

"Do I have time to show Jim my workshop?"

Julian stilled. "My. You *are* honored. Sure, you've got maybe fifteen minutes before breakfast is ready.

Any later than that, and I'm giving your breakfasts to Buster."

At his name, Buster's ears pricked up, and he let out a soft whine.

"I swear that dog understands every word we say." Michael gestured toward the door. "Step this way."

Jim pulled his boots back on and followed him out of the house along the cleared path, past Julian's studio to the identical outbuilding beside it. Jim was burning with curiosity. Michael opened the door and went inside.

Jim had never seen anything like it. The building was the size of a double garage, and around the outer edge of the space stood carvings of bears. The largest had to be five feet high, standing on its rear legs, front paws raised, its mouth open. Jim could almost hear the roar. Other carvings were smaller, and the detail was astounding. But what caught his eye was the lump of wood that stood in the center of the space. It was almost six feet high, and had obviously been a tree trunk, but the bark had been removed, revealing a close-grained wood.

"What are you going to carve from it? Another bear?" Jim walked over to it and stroked its surface. The smell was wonderful.

"Not this one. I'm thinking of a male nude. The proportions would lend themselves perfectly to this piece. Now all I have to find is my model."

Jim laughed. "You can't exactly order one of those from Walmart."

Michael's laughter echoed his. "Correct. But I'll know him when I find him. Then it would simply be a case of taking lots of photos, and I'll work from those." He stroked the wood. "I've not done a nude before, and the idea excites me. It's good to push the envelope from time to time."

"Pushing the envelope is also scary as hell," Jim said quietly.

Michael didn't reply, but Jim was aware of him moving closer. "Anything new is scary, but we all need to grow, right? Stagnation kills creativity."

Jim glanced at his surroundings. "You both have such tremendous talent."

"Thank you." Jim's stomach gave another rumble, and Michael chuckled. "I think that's my cue to feed you."

Jim followed him out of the workshop, and they headed back to the house.

They have it all. Good looks, talent, this beautiful house... And what made it perfect was the happiness they'd obviously found in each other.

For the first time in many years, Jim wanted a taste of what they had.

Michael poured more coffee. "I have to know. What's the next thing for Gary and Mick? I hope you have a really juicy murder for them to solve."

Fuck. Jim didn't know what to say. He didn't want to quash Michael's love of his books by telling him the truth. "Right now I don't have anything planned."

"That's why he came here," Julian said as he buttered a piece of toast. "He's after some inspiration."

He peered at Jim. "I'm right, aren't I? You don't know where to go next, and getting away from it all seemed the perfect solution. Time to clear your mind and come up with some great ideas."

Jim nodded. The fact that Julian had him nailed was no longer a surprise. Julian understood creativity. They both did.

"How well do you know this area?" Michael inquired.

"I know very little," Jim confessed. "I chose the cabin for its solitude."

"Well, if you're looking for inspiration, may I make a suggestion?" Julian sipped his coffee. "Take a look at Yosemite. There is so much to discover."

Jim wasn't so sure about that. He felt comfortable in the cabin, and the thought of driving farther into Yosemite was a little daunting.

"We've lived here for so many years, we know the area well." Michael gave him a thoughtful glance. "Here's an idea. Why don't Julian and I show you the sights?"

"Yes, that's a great idea." Julian nodded enthusiastically.

"I wouldn't want to take you away from your work," Jim protested.

Julian snorted. "Trust me, we both need a break. You'd be doing us a favor. It'd be good to get away from here for a day. And you never know. Inspiration could strike. A change of scenery might be just what you need. What we *all* need."

"Julian's right. Let us do this, please?" Michael's intense gaze met his.

Jim didn't have the heart to refuse. "Okay. When?"

"Tomorrow," Julian said promptly. "We can make

an early start."

Jim laughed. "You don't waste time, do you?" Inside he was buzzing. The idea of spending a day in their company was very pleasant. Then he glanced at Buster. "Is he coming too?"

"Of course. Buster deserves a day out too." Michael reached down to stroke Buster's head. "All those new smells, eh, Buster?"

"More toast?" Julian asked.

Jim patted his stomach. "I couldn't eat another mouthful. In fact, I may not eat again for the rest of the day."

"Are you going to join us for a cocktail this evening?" Michael inquired. "You still have to try Julian's Mai Tai."

"Well, if it's anything like his margaritas, it'll be awesome." Jim liked the idea of sitting around the wood burner, drinking cocktails.

"Great. Seven o'clock, then." Julian beamed. "And then a day of showing you the beauty of Yosemite."

Michael glanced toward the rear of the house, and Jim knew instantly what was going through his mind. "You need to work," he said. "So I'll get out of your hair."

"What hair?" Julian cackled.

Michael speared him with a look. "That *was* you last week, wasn't it? Asking me to shave it all off because you think bald men are sexy?"

"Bald men *are* sexy," Julian retorted. "But you're already sexy." He locked gazes with Michael, and the hairs on Jim's arms stood on end. He didn't think Michael would reach his workshop just yet. In fact, judging by the glances Julian was giving his husband, Jim would lay money they'd be naked before he reached the end of the lane.

What I'd give for someone to look at me *that way.*

It was only as he was walking away from the house that it hit him. It had been a long time since he'd wanted to be the object of someone else's desire. Then another thought struck him, and this one sent his head into a spin.

What I'd give for either of them *to look at me that way.*

Chapter 6

"This is breathtaking!" Jim stared at the vista ahead. They'd driven into the Yosemite Valley, and as they emerged from the Wawona tunnel, Michael had stopped the car. They'd gotten out and walked halfway across a snow-covered bridge before Julian took Jim by the shoulders and turned him to see the view.

"Trust me, it gets better," Julian said with a smile. Jim thought he looked adorable. He wore a sling across his front, from which Buster peered out at their surroundings.

Jim glanced at the slow-moving river beneath them with its lining of ice, the trees with their frosty covering, and the brilliant blue of the sky above. "How can it get better than this?"

Michael chuckled. "Let's see if you're still saying that when we get to the viewpoint."

Jim followed them back to the car, grateful he'd worn his thick jacket, scarf, gloves, and the warmest pair of socks he could find. They drove a short way, then stopped in a large parking lot with only a few cars. Even before he'd gotten out of the car, Jim understood Michael's comment.

That view…

They moved closer to the edge and gazed at the panorama. Trees stretched out before them as far as Jim could see, their tips white with snow, as if someone had shaken flour over them. The snowy peaks rose majestically in the distance, mist floating around their base.

"What am I looking at?"

Julian pointed. "Starting from the left. That's El Capitán, then Half Dome, which is great if you're into tough hikes. That's Glacier Point, and over on the right is Bridalveil. Today we'll go as far as we can in daylight, to give you a taste of the valley."

"It's beautiful." The forest was perfectly framed by the peaks, but what took Jim's breath away was the expanse of sky.

"See what I mean? Talk about inspirational," Julian murmured. "A photo couldn't capture the majesty of it all."

He turned to Michael. "Thank you, both of you. This is incredible."

Michael patted his arm. "You're welcome." He smiled. "Who knows? Maybe Gary and Mick will vacation in Yosemite, and a tourist gets murdered. Then they realize he wasn't just any tourist, he was—"

"Babe? Stop pushing." Julian's eyes sparkled.

Michael's face flushed. "I'm sorry. Here I am, trying to write your next book for you."

Jim laughed. "You're not the first. My publishers tell me they get lots of emails and letters, with suggestions for books. One little old lady even came up with a plot where Gary and Mick visit the UK and get to investigate the attempted assassination of the queen of England." Not that there was going to be a next book for his two detectives. He'd made up his mind on that. There would be no reprieve.

Julian snorted. "Some people have way too much time on their hands."

"Ready for the next view?" Michael inquired.

"I can't wait," Jim replied. He'd chosen Yosemite for its peace and quiet, never dreaming he'd get to see it in all its winter glory.

The company was the icing on the cake.

Julian loved Jim's look of awe as he gazed up at Bridalveil Fall. It was one of Julian's favorite views, and he'd been dying to show it to Jim.

"Doesn't the waterfall freeze at all?" Jim asked, staring at the water force.

"No. It flows year-round. It's only a short hike to the top, but I wouldn't recommend it now. It can get awful slippery."

"Yeah. One time, one of us fell on his butt and slid halfway down the hill. It was a miracle the camera didn't break."

"Yeah, and *one* of us was more concerned with the camera than his husband's sore butt," Julian retorted, giving Michael a hard stare.

Michael grinned. "But I took good care of your butt when we got home, didn't I? In fact, I seem to recall you asking me to take care of it all—"

Julian stopped him with a hand to his mouth. "We've got company, remember?" He removed it slowly.

Michael's grin didn't slip a notch. "He's a writer. I'm pretty sure he can work out the rest of the story."

One glance at Jim's face told him Michael was

correct. That flush was cute.

Jim cleared his throat. "I love the way snow lines the fall and glistens on top of the rocks."

"In spring, the force is so strong, you feel the water breezes from pretty far off." Julian smiled. "I love it like this—the bare cliff face—but as you get close to the falls, there's that covering of snow and the mist that rises."

"Is it lunch time yet?" Michael asked.

"Are we stopping some place to eat?" Jim added.

Julian shook his head. "We've brought food, but only because dining around here costs an arm and a leg. Unless you want pizza in Half Dome Village."

"And we don't," Michael said in a firm tone. "Not when I made us meatloaf sandwiches. Your favorite."

Judging by Jim's smile and the smacking of his lips, meatloaf sandwiches did it for him too.

"I know just the place to eat them too." Julian let out a contented sigh. This was turning out to be a really good day.

Jim drew in a deep breath and let the peace of the place fill him. "I didn't expect this," he murmured, staring at the little red-and-tan chapel nestled in a corner of the Valley floor, standing in the middle of a blanket of white. "How long has it been here?"

"Since the 1870s," Julian informed him. "I love coming here. It feels so peaceful. When I have things to think about, this is where I come. It's a positive place for me."

Jim could understand that.

Julian stroked Buster behind his ears. "And you like it in spring when you get to see all the wildlife, don't you, Buster Bear?"

"Why Buster *Bear*?" Jim asked.

Michael chuckled as he removed folding canvas chairs from the trunk of the car. "Well, seeing as his daddies are bears, it made sense." He flicked a glance in Jim's direction. "And they're not the only ones around here," he added in a low voice.

It took Jim a second or two to realize Michael was referring to him. "Excuse me?"

Julian cleared his throat. "Jim might not know what a bear is, Michael."

It was on the tip of his tongue to say he'd be a poor gay man if he didn't know what a bear was, when Jim remembered he hadn't actually told them he was gay. "Like Michael said, I'm a writer who created a gay couple. Of course I know what a bear is. But… *I'm* no bear." And why he wasn't coming right out and telling then he was gay, he couldn't really say.

Julian snorted. "Have you *looked* in a mirror lately?"

He was shocked into stillness. *That's really how they see me?*

"Of course, compared to us, you're just a baby bear." Michael's eyes twinkled.

Jim was lost for words.

Michael came over to where he stood. "Have I just scrambled your circuits? Honey, you're a gorgeous bear, and if no one's ever told you that, it's about time." He chuckled. "Julian? Get Jim a sandwich, will you? His mouth's open, so he must be hungry."

Julian opened a cool box in the trunk, and handed Jim a wrapped package. "Here." Jim took it, his mind still reeling. Julian gave him an inquiring look, then glanced at Michael. "Babe, you haven't scrambled his circuits—you've fried them." Then he leaned in close, his lips inches from Jim's ear. "He's not the only one who thinks you're gorgeous," he whispered. "And he's right. If no one's ever told you, that is a crying shame." He removed more sandwiches and handed one to Michael with a smile, as if he'd just made a comment on the weather or the scenery, but definitely not a flirtatious statement that rocked Jim's world to its core.

Jim somehow managed to sit, unwrapping his lunch on autopilot. *When was the last time someone made a move on me?* Long enough ago that he couldn't remember it. But to have two of them paying him compliments? Flirting with him?

It crossed his mind for a moment that they were yanking his chain, but then he dismissed the idea. There'd been nothing in their manner to suggest that, and even based on his relatively short acquaintance with them, Jim didn't figure them to be malicious or mean.

That left him with only one conclusion—they were in earnest.

And Jim had no idea how to respond, other than to eat his delicious sandwich in silence, listening to the birds chirping all around them and staring out at the snow-covered landscape.

He knew what lay at the heart of his confusion. He liked them both. He was attracted to them both. But they were a happily married couple, for God's sake. Why were they coming onto him, especially if they thought he was straight?

And what in the hell should he do about it?

"How about we leave the snowy scenes for a while, and relax on a comfy couch in front of a wood burning fireplace with a mug of peppermint hot chocolate?" Michael didn't have to look at Julian to know his eyes had lit up. Julian loved going to the Majestic Hotel.

Jim's mouth fell open, and Michael guessed he wasn't the only one who liked that idea. "That sounds heavenly. I take it such a spot is somewhere along the way?"

Michael smiled. "Now, would I torture you with such a heavenly thing if it weren't possible?"

"Is it far?"

"Only about a mile and a half from Yosemite Village. In fact, we're almost there." He gave Buster a sad glance. "Not you, baby. You get to stay in the car. I don't think they'd accept that you're our service animal."

"Speak for yourself," Julian muttered. "He keeps me sane."

"Will he be okay in the car?" Jim asked anxiously.

That right there was enough to endear him to Michael. "We won't be long. And we'll leave the windows open. Plus, he'll be on his favorite blanket from home."

Julian stroked Buster's head, then kissed it. "Sorry, sweetheart." He glanced at Michael. "Make sure he gets T-R-E-A-T-S when we get home." Buster's ears pricked up, and he laughed. "No, Buster, I'm not buying it. You cannot spell."

"I wouldn't bet on it," Michael muttered as he pulled into the parking lot of the Majestic. They made sure Buster was comfortable on the back seat, then headed into the hotel.

Jim stared at the lobby with wide eyes. "God, it's like being in the Overlook."

Michael could understand that reaction. The couches, the wall hangings, the tall windows, the chandeliers that resembled candles... He chuckled. "If I see Jack Nicholson walking past, we're out of here." He spotted a couple vacating a couch in front of the fireplace, and nudged Julian. "Quick, grab that one."

They sat, and Michael ordered the hot beverages. He settled back against the cushions. "We're almost done for the day."

Jim smiled. "You mean, there's more to see?"

Julian laughed. "We've barely scratched the surface. I can't tell you how many times we've visited the park since we moved here, and each time we see something different."

Jim gave him a speculative glance. "How did you two meet?"

"In a club." He glanced at Michael, his expression neutral.

Michael knew what that look meant—Julian was wondering how much to share about the club.

Jim gazed at Julian thoughtfully. "I see. Seems like it was a fortuitous meeting, if you've been together ever since."

Michael smiled. "It was love at first sight."

Julian chuckled. "He bought me a drink, then another, and then we talked until four in the morning."

"Then I took him back to my place. The rest is history."

Jim shook his head. "You make it sound so simple, but I know few relationships exist like yours. I don't know how you do it. Oh, I know what you said—it's down to patience, compromises and routines—but it has to be more than that." He stared into the fireplace. "You know what I did, when I created Gary and Mick? I took everything I'd seen in all the failing relationships I'd ever known, and I wrote the opposite. I made them the perfect couple. And until recently, I firmly believed such a couple couldn't exist. But you two might have changed my mind on that score."

Michael's stomach clenched. "Hey, whoa there. We're not perfect, believe me. Julian will tell you that too. We've had our bad times, same as any other couple. We just try to work through them."

"We've found what works for us," Julian added. "It doesn't mean our way of life would work for everyone."

Jim frowned. "What does that mean, your 'way of life'?"

At that moment, the server arrived with their mugs of peppermint hot chocolate. When he left them, Michael sighed. "That's a story for another time." He hoped Jim would leave it at that.

Sure enough, Jim fell silent, staring into the flames.

Across from him, Michael caught Julian's steady gaze. After the byplay at the chapel, he knew one thing for certain—they both wanted Jim.

What he was less sure about was if Jim wanted them.

And since when do we make a play for a straight guy? There was only one answer to that—Michael trusted his instincts. And now it seemed Julian was doing the same.

This could get very interesting.

Chapter 7

"Do you think we pushed him too far?" Julian called out as he turned off the shower. He'd been thinking about Jim all day.

Michael's chuckle was audible from the kitchen. "I'm tempted to shout *Squirrel!* That remark came out of nowhere. I take it we're discussing Jim?"

"Yes. I've been thinking about our trip. We haven't seen him for two days. Do you think we've scared him off?" He scrubbed over his head with the towel, then rubbed himself briskly with it before fastening it around his hips.

Michael appeared in the doorway, leaning against it. "I've been wondering about that myself. Maybe he couldn't deal with two guys flirting with him. It *has* been known to happen, right?"

"He didn't run a mile at the time, but maybe he's had time to think on it since, and he's avoiding us. Except…" Julian frowned. "Look, I know I said he's not gay, but—"

"But now your instincts are telling you something different, is that it?"

He nodded. "So what do we do about it?"

Michael said nothing, but removed his phone from his pocket. His finger slid over the screen. Then he looked up with a smile. "Let's see how he responds."

"What did you do?"

"I sent him a text, asking him if he's gay."

Julian gaped. "You didn't."

Michael rolled his eyes. "Honestly, *how* long have you known me? As if I'd do that. I merely invited him for a cocktail. But seeing as it's already six-thirty, I doubt he'll say yes. At least I gave him the opt—" His phone buzzed, and he stared at it. "Well, that answers one question." He raised his head. "So much for avoiding us. He's coming."

Julian sat on the edge of the bed. "Which leaves me not knowing where to go with this. Do we keep our hands off? Do we push him a little more?" Damn it, he wanted to see where this could lead.

"I was right, wasn't I?" Michael got onto the bed behind him, slipping his arms around Julian. "You want him, don't you?"

"That's a rhetorical question, right?" Julian said with a smirk. "About as much as you do."

"Then we'll play this by ear, and see where this evening takes us." Michael nuzzled his neck. "Well, don't *you* smell good?"

Julian shivered. "We… we don't have time for this. He'll be here any minute." Not that his dick was listening to logic. It was already stiffening at the feel of Michael's lips on his skin, Michael's fingers as he played with Julian's nipples. "I *knew* I should've dressed before I spoke to you."

"I'm glad you didn't," Michael murmured. He reached lower to mold his hand around Julian's shaft, the towel doing little to hide his aroused state. Michael's lips brushed over his ear. "We've got time for a little… appetizer, right?"

That was it. Logic and practicality went out the window.

Julian undid his towel, and Michael shifted

instantly off the bed to kneel on the rug between his spread legs. Julian grabbed his cock around the base and held it steady. "Open wide."

Michael's eyes glittered. "Never let it be said I can't follow instructions."

Jim took the Mai Tai Julian had prepared for him, smacking his lips. "I could really get used to this."

Julian laughed. "Which part? Cocktails at seven or my Mai Tais?"

"Both?" Jim settled back against the seat cushions, thoroughly relaxed. Michael sat on the couch facing him, sipping a martini. For the first time since he'd arrived in Yosemite, Jim had a glimmer of an idea. Nothing concrete, but it was a start. He'd spent the day toying with different plots, not yet sold on which one to pursue.

But that's the point to taking this break—to let the ideas flow.

They'd been flowing like molasses in winter thus far.

A fire roared in the wood burner, and Buster lay curled up on his blanket, raising his head occasionally, but not venturing far from the stove.

Julian poured himself a Mai Tai and joined Jim. "We haven't seen much of you the last couple of days. We were beginning to wonder if we'd done something to offend you."

Jim swallowed. "No, you didn't. I was doing a lot of thinking about my writing, that's all. I… I needed to concentrate." That wasn't a lie, but it wasn't the whole truth either. Julian and Michael confused the hell out of him. *And why is he sitting next to me and not Michael?*

"I meant to ask you something about your books," Julian said, placing his glass on the small table at the end of the couch. "When we discovered Michael is your number one fan—" Michael snorted at that, and Julian arched his eyebrows. "You *know* you don't have a leg to stand on in that regard, so hush." He grinned. "Except you'd be the Kathy Bates character, so Jim here wouldn't have two feet to stand on, would he?"

"Julian…." Michael said in a warning tone that even Jim could recognize.

Julian gave him a sweet smile. "*As* I was saying… I asked Michael if there were any… How shall I put this? …sexy times in your books." He grinned. "After all, nowadays sex sells."

Michael coughed. "In case you missed that part, his books sell already."

"But he could sell even more!" Julian remonstrated.

Jim cleared his throat, the answer on the tip of his tongue as it always was when readers got onto the subject of sex. "I gave Gary and Mick their romance, but I kept sex out of it. That would have detracted from the story, which was about the murder, after all. So everything was fade to black. I closed the bedroom door—literally."

"But imagine how your readers would respond if you wrote a novel about Gary and Mick," Julian persisted. "No murder this time, just shifting the book's focus to their personal relationship. Wouldn't that work?"

"I know where you're going with this," Michael interjected. "But you might be pushing things just a little."

"Hey, I'm trying to give Jim here some ideas," Julian retorted. "He says he's looking for ideas, right? Well, I'm just pointing out that sexing up the books might really work."

"And he might not want to sex up his books, did you ever think about that?" Michael speared Julian with a look. "Seeing as I've read every one of them, and you haven't, I might know what I'm talking about. Because they do *not* need to be turned into one-handed books, okay?"

"Did I say that's how they should be?" Julian stared at Michael. "We're not talking *half a book* of sex." He addressed Jim. "That's not what I'm suggesting, believe me. But you could have them constantly touching. Building up the sexual tension between them. Then *bam*—they explode into a passionate scene that burns up the pages *and* their sheets." Julian's eyes gleamed. "Maybe two or three scenes for good measure."

"They're not gonna fuck, okay?" Jim blurted out. The instant the words left his lips, he regretted them. He took a deep breath, trying to calm his climbing pulse. "Look, I'm sorry. I shouldn't have said that, and definitely not the way it came out. You... you hit a nerve, that's all."

Michael sighed heavily. "You have nothing to apologize for." He darted a glance in Julian's direction. "I'd say you have a good case for severe provocation. They're *your* books. You write them as you see fit."

Jim took a long drink of his cocktail, his heartbeat

still fast.

"I'm sorry too." Julian's voice was low. "I had no right to make those suggestions. I guess I went over the top. Michael's right, of course. If your books already sell well, then it's a case of if it ain't broke, don't fix it."

Julian's contrite tone and obvious sincerity soothed him. "I… I wasn't entirely honest with you. I gave you my stock answer about the lack of sex in my books, but that's not the reason why I don't write scenes like that." Another deep breath. "I couldn't write them convincingly, okay? I just don't feel comfortable writing sex."

Michael got up from his couch and came over to sit on Jim's other side. "I read a lot of female authors who write books with gay sex in them. They manage it just fine. As a straight guy, I can understand how it might squick you out."

Jim's heartbeat climbed right back up to its previous level. "Who says I'm straight?" It wasn't as if it was a secret, except to all his readers, of course. And his agent. And his publisher.

Michael stared at him, then leaned across and smacked Julian on the leg. "See? Your gaydar is *way* off. You need to get a refund."

Julian ignored him and gave Jim a puzzled stare. "I don't get it. You're gay?" Jim nodded. "But you're writing about two gay men. So write what you know."

Jim swallowed. "If I wrote that, believe me, it wouldn't make good reading."

"Oh God." Julian's eyes widened. "You're… you're not a virgin, are you?"

That raised a smile. "No, I'm not. I'm just celibate. And you already know why, because I kind of hinted at it when we were at that hotel."

"You said you've seen a lot of bad relationships?" Michael said.

Jim nodded. "I don't like complications, so... I avoid them. I've gotten used to distancing myself from emotions and physical encounters. Plus, I have a really low tolerance for bullshit, so I don't often engage with people."

"You engage with us," Michael commented.

"Yes, that's true. But then again, I've never met a couple like you." He glanced at Julian. "What would be so bad if I were a virgin?"

"Oh, it wouldn't be *bad*." Julian's eyes sparkled. "I've enjoyed popping a few cherries in my time. No, in *your* case, it would just be unbelievable."

Jim stilled. "Excuse me?"

Julian's smile lit up his face. "Honey, I *told* you how gorgeous you are. What I didn't mention is how much I've been longing to do this." And before Jim could ask what this was, Julian's hand was on his cheek, and Julian was kissing him on the mouth, slow and sensual.

What the fuck?

Jim reared back, freeing himself from Julian's embrace, swallowing hard. Julian's lips had felt wonderful, but that wasn't the point. Michael was sitting *right there*.

Julian gazed at him steadily. "You liked that."

"You could've asked first," he blurted.

"But where's the fun in that?" Julian's eyes held amusement.

Jim jerked his head to stare at Michael. "How... how can you just... sit there?"

Michael nodded. "You're right, of course. I should be pissed. Which I am. He got to kiss you first. And now I want *my* turn."

Before Michael could continue, Jim lurched to his feet. "I don't understand what's going on here." His head was spinning.

"What is there to understand?" Julian gave him a puzzled glance. "Or are three-ways not dreamed of in your philosophy, Mr. Writer?" His lips twitched.

"Please, Jim, sit down," Michael urged him.

His heart pounding, Jim sat. He wanted to know more. He wanted to understand. "You've been together twenty-five years. You're a happily married couple. Or do I have it all wrong, and it's just an act? Are you really falling apart, and you're papering over the cracks with sexual encounters with others?"

"Not at all," Michael said warmly. "We have a great marriage."

"We've seen a lot of relationships fail too," Julian admitted. "Ours has lasted because of those three things I told you about—communication, expectations, and honesty."

"Honesty?" Jim felt lost. "So this is what you meant the other day when you mentioned your 'way of life.'" Now the comment made sense.

Michael nodded. "We've always known sex is important to us. But we saw no reason to deny ourselves if someone came along who… interested us."

"We have one rule," Julian said. "We only play if we're together. So if a guy—or guys—come along, and there's obviously something there, a spark of attraction, lust, call it what you will—then we invite them to play."

"No strings. No complications. They know from the outset that it's just a fleeting thing. It's meant to be fun. We enjoy each other, and then they leave." Michael added.

"We don't go *looking* for such men," Julian insisted.

"In fact, if we only had sex with each other for the rest of our days, that would be just fine."

"This works for us," Michael said emphatically. "Jealousy is not a factor as long as we're open and honest with each other, and with the men who come into our lives."

"Michael's right. We have a great marriage. And both of us being open about what we want is what *makes* it great." Julian locked gazes with Jim. "And right now… we want you."

"But only if that's what you want too," Michael said quickly.

Jim had no idea what he wanted.

He rose to his feet again. "I have to go." His thoughts raced, his heart hammered, and something fluttered deep in his belly. Heat threatened to overwhelm him, and his chest felt tight.

"Please, don't—"

Michael held up a hand to silence Julian before meeting Jim's gaze. "It's okay. If you're uncomfortable, of course you must go." His face fell. "I'm sorry if we've ruined things."

Jim couldn't speak. He headed for the door, squirmed into his boots, and pulled on his coat. Without a word, he was out of there, almost running along the lane, the night air biting into his exposed skin. Moonlight provided just enough illumination to light his way.

What the hell?

He slowed a little, trying to get himself under control, his mind well and truly blown. *Did that just happen?* He kept replaying Julian's kiss in his head. *Fuck.* He could still feel those warm lips on his. He could hear the soft sigh Julian made, the touch of his hand on

Jim's face. And dear God, the *promise* in that kiss…

As he came to the cabin, he stopped dead in front of it, and stared into the night sky, doing his best to calm his mind and look at the situation with a clear head.

Is it so bad, what they have? They're honest about it. Jim knew such relationships existed, sure, but he'd always assumed they were doomed to fail. Jealousy was certain to raise its ugly head. But here were Michael and Julian, telling him the opposite.

He turned to stare in the direction of their house.

Could it work?

Except he'd already seen the answer to that question for himself. It plainly worked for them.

And what about them wanting me?

Jim took a couple of steps away from the cabin, shivering. *I wanted them to look at me the way they look at each other.* He'd have been a liar if he denied part of him wanted what they were offering. The thought was enough to have him heading for the lane once more.

Then he stopped and stood in the semi-blackness of the forest, the moonlight etching the outlines of the trees in silver.

But what are *they offering? They don't want a relationship, just sex with no strings. Two sexy guys are offering to fuck me, with no complications. When we're done, and I leave here, that's it. No adverse consequences.*

He froze. It couldn't be that simple—could it?

He turned to gaze at the cabin. *I should turn in for the night. I should leave this alone.*

Except deep down, he knew he didn't want to do that.

If I did this… I'd have to make a rule of my own. If it starts feeling weird, we stop. After all, they had their rule, so why shouldn't he have his?

Then Jim realized he was facing in the direction of their house again. It seemed as if his subconscious was giving him a push.

I guess I've made up my mind.

He set off for the house at a brisk pace, partly because of the cold, but mostly for fear that if he took his time, he'd change his mind again before he reached them.

He walked up to the side porch and rang the doorbell, his heart doing a frantic dance. *This isn't a mistake, is it? Am I doing the right thing? What if—*

Michael appeared at the door, his eyes wide. He opened it. "Hey."

Jim took a deep breath and stepped out of his comfort zone. "Can we try this again, please?"

Chapter 8

A faint frown creased Michael's brow. "Oh. We didn't think we'd see you again this evening. Julian's just putting out the dinner."

As far as Jim was concerned, that was a sign. "I'm sorry. I won't disturb you." He turned to go, perturbed to realize he was shaking a little. All that internal conflict, all the mental to-ing and fro-ing, and it came down to bad timing.

"Wait, please!"

Jim stopped and glanced back. Michael beckoned him to enter the house. "There's plenty. It's only a casserole, but Julian's a great cook. Please, eat with us?"

Jim deliberated for a moment. "I don't want to be an imposition."

Michael gave him a warm smile. "You could never be that. Now get in here before my nuts freeze and drop off, Julian sprays them with copper paint, and uses them as Christmas tree decorations."

"Wow. That's pretty graphic." He chuckled. "Well, we can't have that." He stepped into the warm interior and removed his boots. Michael helped him out of his coat and hung it up once more. Jim could smell the casserole, its aroma drifting through the house, and his stomach rumbled.

"Babe? Another place at the table." Michael's hand was on Jim's back, gentle and comforting. "We've got company." His voice was as warm as his smile.

Julian appeared with all the speed of a Jack-in-a-box, his eyes lighting up when he spied Jim. "Oh, thank God."

Jim grinned. "What, no naked man apron tonight?"

Julian laughed. "I'm pretty sure I'll have a naked man on me at some point this evening." Then he disappeared from view. "Come and get it!" he hollered.

"He means dinner, right?" Jim joked.

Michael rubbed his back, and the gesture was soothing. "I am *so* happy you came back. For the moment, let's enjoy the food, and maybe some good conversation."

Jim had gotten this far, he didn't want to take a step backward now. His heartbeat quickened. "I... I might be up for a little more than just conversation." It had been a long time since he'd been physical with a guy, and never with two, so he really was playing this by ear.

Michael's eyes gleamed. "Whatever you want, okay? Your rules for tonight."

That eased his quaking heart a little. "Okay." He followed Michael into their dining room, where Julian was pouring red wine into the glasses.

He held up the bottle. "Would you like some?"

"Sure." Jim took the chair Michael pulled out for him, and sat. "This smells wonderful." Dinner was so far removed from what he'd imagined would happen, and yet it was perfect.

"Just a little something I threw together. Beef, onions, red wine, garlic..."

"My mouth is already watering." Jim waited as Julian ladled casserole into a deep bowl, while he helped himself to a hunk of bread that smelled awesome. He glanced at the floor. "Why isn't Buster here, begging with those cute puppy dog eyes?"

Julian snorted. "Because he knows if he does that, there will be no treats for a *very* long time."

"What Julian forgets to add is that sometimes he forgets the rules, and uses Buster like a little vacuum cleaner," Michael added. "Now eat while he isn't around."

That first mouthful was heaven, and Jim couldn't hold back the soft moan of pleasure.

Michael nodded, smiling. "Aren't I a lucky man? He paints, he cooks, he cleans…"

"And I'm pretty good in the sack too," Julian added, his eyes twinkling.

Jim loved the way Michael locked gazes with Julian. "'Pretty good'? How about, goddamn amazing?"

Julian reached for Michael's hand, lifted it to his lips, and kissed his knuckles.

Jim had never been met a couple so obviously besotted with each other after so many years together. *Maybe that's because I've been around the wrong guys.* "You two inspire me," he said quietly.

"To do what?" Julian asked, a playful note in his voice.

Jim took a sip of wine. "I need to be honest with you. Especially you, Michael." When Michael gave him a puzzled glance, Jim sighed. "You asked me a few days ago what I had planned for Gary and Mick. That book I sent off last week? It's the last book for them. The very last."

Michael's jaw dropped. "You're… you're killing them off?"

Jim nodded. "I thought about it a lot, and I came to the conclusion that I didn't want to write those books anymore. I wanted to try something different.

That's why I came here. I needed inspiration. The only problem was, nothing came. No epiphanies. No shiny new book ideas. And then I met you two."

"You could write about us," Julian teased.

Michael hushed him before giving Jim his full attention. "Wow," he said, his hand to his chest. "Firstly, I have to say I'm heartbroken to know there'll be no more murders to solve. But they're your books. And secondly, I'm intrigued. How have we inspired you?"

"You'll laugh." Jim had certainly laughed out loud when the idea had first come to him. It was so… out there.

Michael's expression grew solemn. "I won't laugh."

"Neither will I," Julian said quickly.

Jim took another mouthful of wine. "I've been toying with the idea of writing… gay fiction. Where the central characters are gay, and the story revolves around them—their lives, their experiences, their loves…" He bit back a smile. "There might even be a bit of romance in there." He resumed eating, feeling more at ease. It was a relief to let it out.

"I think it's a great idea," Michael said with a beaming smile. "A whole new genre to conquer."

His enthusiasm was the balm Jim needed to soothe his fears. "Thank you for the vote of confidence."

They lapsed into silence as they ate, but it was a comfortable silence. Jim felt relaxed, his inner turmoil of earlier forgotten. When they'd finished, Julian gestured to the living room. "Why don't you go and sit by the stove while I make the coffee?" He cocked his head. "Unless you want to dash off."

Jim smiled. "I'm in no hurry to leave."

The light in Julian's eyes did wonders for his ego.

"Great. Then go sit. I'll be right in." He glanced at Michael. "And you? Take care of our guest. I think you've got some catching up to do."

Michael's sharp intake of breath told Jim he'd just missed something important.

He followed Michael into the living room, and Buster got up from his blanket to come over. Jim crouched to greet the little dog. "Hey there." He scritched behind Buster's ears. "How's my favorite dog?"

"That's sweet." Michael sat on the sofa.

"I mean it. He's adorable. And such a good dog too. You didn't beg for bits of your daddies' dinner." He gave Buster's back a rub, and Buster rolled over to show his fuzzy tummy. Jim sighed. "No one loves you like a dog."

Buster licked his hand as if in reply.

Michael patted the seat cushion next to him, in the middle of the sofa. "Sit here."

Jim's heart decided to quicken again. He joined Michael, perched on the edge of the seat, but Michael laid a hand to his shoulder and firmly pushed him back. "Now, where were we?" Michael whispered, right before he leaned over and took Jim's mouth in a chaste kiss.

As first kisses went, it was sweet. And then Michael tugged gently on Jim's bottom lip with his teeth, and everything changed. Michael's hand was on Jim's neck, stroking him, and his tongue was in Jim's mouth, exploring him.

Jim let out a low moan, and Michel pulled back instantly. "Too much?"

Jim shook his head. "Not enough." And then he cradled Michael's head in his hand, drawing him into a kiss that sent warmth surging through him. Michael rubbed Jim's short hair, trailing his fingers lower to stroke his thumb along Jim's bearded jaw, while he sucked on Jim's tongue, sending shivers of desire trickling through him.

The sofa dipped, and suddenly there was a warm mouth on Jim's neck, kissing down it, and Jim's shivers doubled.

"You smell so good," Julian murmured. He flicked Jim's earlobe with his tongue, and Jim shuddered. The little bit of flesh right below there was a hot spot Jim had almost forgotten, and Julian homed in on it like a heat-seeking missile, sucking him there, his hand on Jim's chest, his thumb rubbing over Jim's nipple through his sweater.

"Aw, fuck," Jim murmured into Michael's kiss, shuddering out a sigh when Michael's hand joined Julian's. Then Michael's lips were on his neck, and Julian was claiming his mouth, both of them making soft murmurs that told Jim they were enjoying this as much as he was.

Julian reached under the hem of his sweater. "Can I?"

Jim loved that he asked. "God, yes," he groaned as Michael sucked harder on his neck. There was going to be a mark in the morning, and Jim wanted it. He wanted to remember the intimacy of the moment, the low noises of pleasure and arousal, the feel of Julian's fingers on his bare skin after he'd tugged Jim's T-shirt free of his waistband and was stroking his belly beneath the sweater in languid circles, moving higher, higher, higher...

Jim gasped, then moaned as Julian gripped his nipple and gave it a little twist.

How the fuck did he know? There had been no clues, nothing he'd said to them, yet Julian had somehow seen Jim's need. He groaned when Julian roughly pushed up both T-shirt and sweater until they were under his chin, then clamped his mouth to Jim's nipple. Michael's mouth on his muffled the sound, no sweet, tender kiss now but a more forceful one, a demanding, passionate, toe-curling kiss that sent heat pulsing through him in wave after wave.

Then Michael's hand strayed to Jim's crotch, and Jim knew he'd reached his limit. "Stop, please."

It was like flicking a switch. Both men sat back, both a bit breathless, their pupils large and dark, their faces flushed.

"Too fast?" Michael looked Jim in the eye, his hand gentle on Jim's stomach, resting there.

Julian stroked Jim's cheek. "You okay?"

Jim shivered. "Overload, I think." He drew in a couple of deep breaths to calm his trembling body. "Please… don't think I was leading you on, or—"

Michael silenced him with a finger to his lips. "Hush. It's okay. And neither of us thinks that." He removed his finger, and leaned in to kiss Jim's cheek. Jim let out a sigh of relief.

Julian nodded. "How long has it been since you made out with someone?"

Jim let out a wry chuckle. "Long enough that I don't remember?" And that had been *one* guy.

Making out with two guys threatened to blow his mind.

Except now that he'd drawn an abrupt close to their make-out session, he felt awkward as fuck. "Maybe I should go," he suggested, pulling his sweater down to cover his bare skin. How in the hell was he supposed to act after stopping them all in mid-action?

Michael covered Jim's hand with his own. "You can go on a couple of conditions."

Jim blinked. "And what are those?"

Michael's gaze locked onto his. "That you don't stay away because you feel awkward. I would hate for that to happen."

"Me too," Julian murmured.

"And… if you feel you want to continue this, you let us know. We're not going to push you," Michael affirmed.

Then Julian leaned over and kissed him. "And we're not going to stop wanting you either," he whispered.

Jim swallowed. "I'll… remember that." He got to his feet, and they got up with him. "Thank you for dinner."

Julian grinned. "Thank *you* for the dessert."

"Dessert? What—*Oh.*" Jim's cheeks warmed. "You're welcome."

"It was rather delicious dessert," Michael said in a low, sexy voice that did something to Jim's insides. "Feel free to share that again. Anytime."

"Only, preferably not when he's working and he's holding a chisel," Julian added, his eyes twinkling. "I'd stay clear at those times."

Jim chuckled. "Got it."

They accompanied him to the door, and once he'd put on his boots, Michael helped him into his coat, buttoning it up. "Do we get a goodnight kiss?"

Jim nodded, his heart racing a little at the thought of Michael's lips on his again. Then *two* mouths took his, and Jim went with it, amazed that a three-way kiss was even possible.

Julian stroked Jim's cheek once more. "Yup, I was right. You are something very special, Jim Traynor." He opened the door, and Jim stepped out into the cold night air. Michael and Julian waved to him as he walked briskly toward the lane, and then they were gone.

Jim hurried back to his cabin, his mind replaying the scene in a loop. He wanted to get to his laptop and write in his journal. He wanted to remember everything while it was still fresh.

He also knew it wouldn't be long before he would go back for more.

Chapter 9

Michael switched off the bathroom light and walked naked into the bedroom. Julian was already in bed, lying on his back, his gaze focused on the ceiling. Michael came to a halt at the foot of the bed, waiting for Julian to notice his erection.

It wasn't as if he could miss it. Michael's shaft was like steel.

Nothing. Not even a glance.

Michael cleared his throat, and Julian propped himself up on his elbows. "Did I miss something?" Michael gave the merest flick of his head down to his crotch. Julian smiled. "Is that for me?"

"It will be—as soon as you tell me where your head was just now."

To his surprise, Julian returned to his previous position. "I was thinking, that's all."

Michael climbed onto the bed and crawled up to where Julian lay beneath the comforter. "Now I'm *really* worried." He pressed his hand to Julian's brow. "Well, you haven't got a fever."

Julian frowned. "What *are* you talking about?"

Michael bit his lip. "Since when do you ignore my dick when it's being offered to you? Unless you're ill. Mind you, there *was* that time you had—"

Julian stopped his words with a finger to Michael's lips. "I was thinking about Kristofer, if you must know."

The name was enough to rob Michael of all his intentions.

He froze. "Whatever made you think of him?" Neither of them had mentioned his name for years. It wasn't a conscious decision on Michael's part not to discuss him, but rather a form of self-preservation.

It still hurt to remember him.

He got under the comforter and lay on his side next to Julian, reaching out to stroke his beard. "Babe?" When no response was forthcoming, Michael cupped Julian's chin. "Talk to me."

"Maybe it's because of Jim," Julian suggested.

It didn't take a genius to work out why.

"He does have something of Kristofer about him, doesn't he?" Not that it had been obvious at first. It had taken Jim's reaction to their shared kiss to bring home just how similar the two men were.

"Christ, Michael." Julian shivered. "The noises he made. The way he shuddered when I played with his nipples. That deer-in-the-headlights look when he let himself go, just a little, as if he were only then realizing how good it could be."

Oh God. Julian could have been talking about both of them.

Michael tugged Julian into his arms and held him close. Julian buried his face in Michael's chest, and Michael's heart sank to feel the quiet sobs that wracked his body. It would have been easy to share Julian's grief—not that it had ever left Michael—but he'd made up his mind a long time ago: grief was *not* a place to stay, and one of them had to be strong.

He stroked Julian's head, kissing him there. "Oh, baby. I know. But this is why we stick to casual, right? This is why we're happy with guys who come and go.

Because we can't go through that again." That would wreck them.

Julian craned his neck to look Michael in the eye. "I loved him, you know? I fucking *loved* Kristofer."

Michael kissed his forehead. "I know, babe. Me too. But we had to let him go, right?"

Julian's eyes blazed. "That fucker Ray didn't give us any choice."

Michael cupped Julian's cheek. "Think about it. How would *you* feel if you met someone, fell passionately in love with them, wanted to build a life with them—and then discovered your future partner has a couple of Daddies? Ray wasn't into open relationships."

"Do you think it broke Kristofer's heart like it broke ours?" Julian wiped his eyes with his hand. "I would hate to think of him being miserable."

"I know." Michael tightened his arms around Julian. "But we did what we promised we'd do. We severed all lines of communication. We haven't checked up on him." Another gentle kiss to Julian's forehead. "We can only hope and pray he's happy."

"You don't regret coming here, do you?" Julian murmured against his chest.

Michael sighed. "No, baby, I don't. I love what we have here."

"And you don't think we were... running away?"

That was a tricky one. "I think we came here originally to lick our wounds in peace, and to put him far away from our thoughts." Not that it had worked out like that initially. Kristofer had moved with them. He was in their hearts, after all. But with each passing year, the pain of losing him had dulled from a sharp lance to a dull ache.

"And you're happy with how we live?"

Michael hadn't seen this insecure side of Julian for a long time, and it grieved him. He'd truly believed they'd moved on. "What you said to Jim was the truth," Michael assured him.

Julian sniffed. "Which bit? I've said a lot of things since we met him."

"That if we only had sex with each other for the rest of our days, that would be just fine."

Julian rolled onto his back, tugging Michael to lie on top of him. "You believe that too?"

Michael smiled. "With all my heart." He closed the gap between them, and kissed Julian softly on the lips. "I love you."

Julian looped his arms around Michael's neck, his eyes shining. "Love you too." He hooked his legs around Michael's waist. "I think there's someplace you need to be," he whispered.

"And where's that?" Michael rolled his hips, sliding his dick over Julian's shaft, loving the way Julian's breathing caught.

Julian cupped Michael's nape, drawing him down into a kiss. "Inside me," he murmured against Michael's lips.

Michael kissed him, then pressed his hand over Julian's heart. "I thought I already was."

Jim woke to the sound of birdsong after a night of uninterrupted sleep. He stretched beneath the comforter, content to lie there and enjoy the warmth.

Isn't it amazing how good a little making out can make you feel? God, if they could bottle this feeling, someone could make a fortune. He closed his eyes, and he was right back there, sandwiched between them, Michael's lips on his, Julian's on his neck. Jim grasped his dick and gave it a slow pull, focusing his thoughts on the memory of Julian's mouth on his nipple, hot and wet. And that little twist Julian had given the taut tiny nub…

His hand moved faster, his thoughts now locked onto the three of them, only this time, Michael rubbed his hand over Jim's crotch, and Jim didn't stop him. He tugged harder, imagining Michael's warm fingers sliding beneath his waistband, seeking his burgeoning cock, stroking it.

Oh fuck. Then there were *two* hands around his shaft, working in tandem, and Jim knew he was a hair's breadth away from coming. Try as he might, he couldn't hold it back, and he creamed his fingers, his belly quivering, his breathing loud in the quiet cabin.

There was nothing like having to clean up to get a man out of bed.

By the time he was on his second mug of coffee, Jim's mind was awash with ideas. The prospect of writing in a new genre filled him with excitement rather than trepidation, and he wanted to hold onto that feeling. He opened the door to his balcony, then sat in one of the chairs, a thick blanket over him, his notebook in his lap. With no fixed idea for a plot, he wrote whatever came into his head. It was a cathartic experience, letting his mind run free, not putting a block on anything that occurred to him.

It was also something he'd never done before in all his years of writing.

"Well, hello there," Michael called out from below.

Jim threw off his blanket and peered over the balcony. Michael stood there in his thick jacket, Buster sniffing the ground around his feet. "Did Buster bring you here, or was it the other way around this time?" Jim teased.

"I took a break. Besides, Buster was due for a walk." Michael smiled. "You got any coffee going? Stupid question, I know, because don't all writers live on coffee? But I'd love a cup if you've got some."

Jim chuckled. "I was about to brew a fresh pot. Come on up." An outright lie, but he wasn't averse to more coffee. He set up the machine, pausing when a small wiry dog dashed across the cabin with a happy-sounding yap. Jim crouched to greet him. "Hi there, Buster. Smell anything interesting on the way here?"

Michael laughed as he stepped into the kitchen area. "A rabbit, but it escaped." He glanced around the cabin.

It was the first time Michael had appeared ill at ease, and Jim was intrigued. He gestured to the couch. "Take a seat. The coffee won't be long." Now that Michael was there, Jim felt a bit awkward. It had been too long since Jim had had to observe the niceties of post-making-out conversation.

"I'm not here to push," Michael said as he sat, Buster instantly heading for his lap. "I said we wouldn't do that." He met Jim's gaze. "You don't feel awkward about last night, do you?"

Jim went with the truth. "I'm just not sure what to say. I mean, what do you say to someone who had their tongue down your throat?" he quipped.

"Thank you?" Michael suggested, his lips twitching. He seemed to relax a little.

Jim stared at him for a second before bursting into laughter. "Yeah, that *is* one way to go." The coffee dripped into the pot, and there was no way Jim was going to stand next to it, waiting. He joined Michael on the couch. "What are you working on?"

Michael gave a wry smile. "To be honest, nothing at the moment. I keep scouring the Internet for some inspiration for that piece I told you about—the nude? But so far, I haven't had any luck."

"Any ideas what kind of a piece you'd like to do?" Jim asked. "I mean, will he be standing, brushing his teeth, sitting on the toilet…" He chuckled. "I can't see many people wanting to *buy* that, however."

"Again, I have nothing specific in mind." Michael glanced at Jim's notebook on the countertop. "What about you? Have you gotten any more ideas about your next book?"

Jim laughed. "Tons of them, most of which I probably won't use. But at least they're coming to me now."

"That's down to us." Michael preened. "We obviously got your creative juices flowing."

It was on the tip of Jim's tongue to reveal to Michael exactly *what* they'd gotten flowing that morning. "Am I still invited for cocktails this evening?"

Michael beamed. "Of course you are. In fact…" His eyes sparkled. "You have an open invitation to come over anytime you like. Don't wait to be asked."

"But… you both have work to do." Jim cocked his head to one side as the implication sank in. "Does *everyone* you take an… interest in, receive the same invitation?" He was under no illusions. There had to have been a lot of guys before him who'd caught the eyes of their hosts.

Michael slowly shook his head. "Just you."

Jim swallowed. "And this is what you call no pushing?"

"Fuck." Michael ran his hand over his head. "I'm trying my damnedest here not to say what's really on my mind."

"Why?" Jim's heartbeat sped up.

A groan fell from Michael's lips. "Because I don't want to fuck this up, okay? I don't want to scare you off. *We* don't want to scare you off."

Jim grabbed his courage with both hands. "Try me."

Michael sat so still beside him. Buster pricked up his ears, as if he sensed Michael's mood. "I'm sorry," he said at last. "I had no right to say any of that. It's not fair. You're not here on vacation, you're here to work, and I shouldn't drag you away from—"

"Michael, for Christ's sake, spit it out!" The words came out louder and harsher than he'd intended, but he had to know.

That wrung another groan from Michael. "I want to take you back to our place, strip you naked, and get you in our bed. And then I want the three of us to spend the rest of the day fucking. It's all I've thought about since I woke up this morning." He locked gazes with Jim. "Which is why I haven't gotten anything done." A long sigh shuddered out of him.

Jim fought to maintain his calm. Michael's raw words lit a fuse inside him, and although his heart was hammering, he didn't want to put out the fire spreading through his body. He took a deep breath. "Then how about I switch off the coffee machine, put on my coat, and we walk over there?"

They had to go *now, right this second* before his brain kicked in and tried to change his mind.

The hitch in Michael's breathing and the dilation of his pupils said more than words ever could. Jim got up from the couch, shut everything off in the kitchen, locked the doors to the balcony, and grabbed his boots and jacket.

I can't believe I'm doing this.

Now all he had to do was get his heart to calm the fuck down.

Chapter 10

As they approached the house, Michael got out his phone and touched the screen. He gave Jim a smile. "Want to know how much we both want this? Watch this." He brought the phone to his ear. "Babe? Yes, I know you're working... *Babe*... Jim is with me. So how do you feel about taking a day away from your canvas and spending it in our bed?"

Seconds later, the door to Julian's studio flew open and Julian tossed his white lab coat aside before striding toward them. "Work can wait."

Despite his churning stomach and tightening chest, Jim chuckled. "I'm flattered." Then his heart pounded as Julian walked straight up to him and kissed him, not even trying to rein in his obvious need, reaching around Jim to cup his ass and squeeze it. Jim moaned into the kiss. "Can... can we take this inside?"

Michael laughed. "Julian. Down boy. Let him breathe."

Julian released him, his eyes shining. He locked gazes with Jim. "You sure about this?"

Jim pushed out a nervous laugh. "No?" Then Michael took Jim's hand in his, and damn, that felt good.

"We'll take things as slow as you like," Michael assured him. "But right now, I just want to hold you."

Fuck. Jim found his courage. "Then take me to your bed, because I want that too."

Julian opened the door, and Buster followed them inside, tail wagging, jumping up at Julian's legs. Jim bent to pat his head. Michael scooped Buster into his arms. "Sorry, Buster Bear. This is one of those times when you get to stay on your bed." He put the little dog down, and Buster trotted back to his spot by the fireplace.

Jim was kind of glad about that. It would feel too much as if they had a spectator, and Jim's insides were already quivering, his heart hammering.

Maybe taking it slow was the perfect way to go.

"Is it me, or did Buster understand every word you just said?" he joked.

Julian laughed. "We say the same thing. But he knows the score. No furry interlopers when his daddies are... busy."

"Can we stop talking and get our clothes off?" Michael's impatience was gratifying.

They all removed their boots, leaving them by the door, and Julian helped Jim out of his jacket. He followed them into the living room, where they stopped. Julian gave Michael a keen glance.

Michael nodded. "Okay, before we go any further..." He went over to the desk in the corner, opened a drawer, and removed a plastic document wallet. He brought it over to Jim, who took it with a frown.

"What's this?" He glanced at the top sheet, and caught his breath. "Oh."

"The results of our latest tests, which were done two weeks ago." Julian met Jim's gaze. "This is just to confirm we're healthy."

Jim cleared his throat. "Okay... my latest physical was last month. Nothing to report there either." His pulse raced. Everything had just gotten a little more real.

Michael's hand was gentle on his arm. "We both take PrEP. And we're sharing all this because we don't like condoms. But if that's a deal-breaker, then tell us now, and we'll use them."

Holy fuck. It was years since Jim last had sex, but he'd never once done it without a glove. What shocked him was that the thought of going bare was a turn-on. "I... that's okay with me." His voice cracked.

Julian smiled. "It's okay to be honest if you'd rather use protection. We really won't mind." He stepped closer and cupped Jim's chin, locking him into an intense gaze. "I just want you to feel comfortable."

Jim shivered. "It's been a while, all right? And I know what they say about riding a bike... that you never forget..." He wasn't so sure.

"You haven't forgotten how to kiss, that's for certain." Michael's eyes gleamed. "So why don't we take this to our bedroom, and make out a little?"

Jim really liked that idea. "Lead the way." His heart still pounding, he followed Julian around a corner to the stairs that led to the mezzanine. Michael was behind him, and below, Buster let out a soft whine.

Julian paused at a door, and Jim gazed at him inquiringly. Julian gave a wry chuckle. "Would it surprise you to know you're not the only one who's nervous?"

Jim blinked. "But... why?" *They do this a lot, right?*

Julian took a deep breath. "I've been thinking about this ever since that trip to Yosemite. It's kind of a big deal for me."

"For both of us," Michael added. Then he pushed the door open, grabbed Jim's hand, and led him into a large room with a high sloping ceiling, three huge windows set into it. In the center against the highest wall was a wide bed that had to be seven feet across. Mounds of pillows sat against the headboard, and there were slender wooden pillars at each corner, a wooden frame crowning them. The comforter was a gorgeous shade of mossy green that went perfectly with the pale green walls. Sunlight spilled into the bedroom, creating an airy space.

At the far end was a doorway that Jim assumed led to a bathroom.

Michael pointed to it. "If you want to use it, go ahead."

It was as if he'd read Jim's mind. "Thank you." Hopefully there'd be a towel to cover himself with.

"Just don't walk out of there naked, okay?" Julian's lips twitched. "That's our job."

Apparently, Julian was a mind reader too.

Jim crossed the floor, went into the bathroom, and closed the door behind him. Almost instantly, soft music filtered from the main room, low and melodic. It eased Jim's racing heart, and he took several deep breaths. He knew why his stomach had an invasion of butterflies—his first three-way, first time bareback, first sex in *eons*—but he also knew deep down that Michael and Julian would follow his lead.

They'll make it good for me. The thought brought its own measure of calm.

A couple of minutes later, he left the bathroom and stopped dead at the sight before him. Michael and Julian were on the bed, still clothed, kissing and touching each other, and their low noises of pleasure were audible above the music. Jim watched them, entranced by their tenderness and obvious love for each other.

Then he realized he was about to be on the receiving end of that same tenderness, and warmth flooded through him.

Michael paused and beckoned him over. "Come here." He and Julian parted, making space between them, and Jim clambered onto the bed, shuffling up until he lay on his back in the center. Michael gave him a warm smile. "I am *so* happy you're here." Before Jim could tell him he felt the same way, Michael claimed Jim's mouth in a lingering kiss, and Julian wasted no time inching his fingers beneath Jim's sweater, stroking his belly.

"This feels really decadent," Jim murmured between kisses, stifling a moan when Julian pushed up his sweater and tweaked his nipples.

Michael chuckled against his neck. "Are you usually a have-sex-at-night-with-the-light-off kinda guy?

Jim laughed, then shivered as Michael kissed him below his ear. "Okay, guilty as charged."

Julian kissed his belly. "Then allow us to educate you on the illicit thrill of spending daylight hours between the sheets." He raised his head and met Jim's gaze. "For starters, you're wearing way too much clothing." His eyes sparkled. "So let's do something about that." He unbuckled Jim's belt, and that was enough to send Jim's pulse rocketing. When Michael pulled him upright and tugged at his sweater, Jim decided this was no time for nerves. He *wanted* this, dammit, so maybe he should let himself enjoy it to the full.

"What about your clothes?" he demanded.

Michael laughed. "They're coming off next."

It wasn't long before they were all naked, and Jim

drank in the sight of them. Michael's chest was broader than Julian's, but with less hair. Both men had thick cocks, though Michael's was the longer of the two. Julian was the stockier man, with muscled arms and thighs. It was then that Jim realized his first impression had been correct.

He was sharing a bed with two bears, and dealing with an inferiority complex.

"Look at you." Michael's voice held unmistakable awe. "Kneel up for me." Jim complied, trembling slightly at the feel of Michael's hand on his ass. "Look how pretty that is."

Julian joined him, gently squeezing his ass cheek before moving to the front to curl his fingers around Jim's dick. "I think this is just as pretty. Looks like it will hit the spot too." He leaned in and kissed Jim on the lips, and all of a sudden two pairs of arms enveloped him.

It was heady as fuck, and they hadn't even gotten started yet.

"You two sure know how to make a guy feel good," he murmured.

Julian stilled. "You're beautiful, sweetheart." He rubbed his hand over Jim's closely cut hair, moving down his neck, and ending up at his bearded jawline. Julian kissed him there, and Michael was at Jim's other side, his lips laying a trail of kisses down his neck to his collarbones.

Fuck, Jim wanted to run his hands over both of them.

"Lie down," Michael said in a low voice, pulling on Jim's arm.

Michael stretched out beside him, cradling Jim's shoulders in his arm while they kissed some more.

Julian's mouth was warm on Jim's belly and chest, and Jim shuddered when he teased Jim's nipples with teeth and tongue.

"You get to touch too, you know," Michael murmured against his lips.

That was all the invitation Jim needed. He stroked Julian's short hair, shivering with each tug on his nipples. His other hand went to Michael's nape, exerting a little pressure as their kiss deepened. When Julian traced the length of his cock with his fingertips, Jim made a grunt of approval. He didn't know what felt best—Michael's lips, the way he cradled Jim as though he were something precious, Julian's teasing tongue, or the way he stroked Jim's shaft.

Jim had never been so hard.

Julian raised his head. "I have to taste this." He squeezed Jim's solid cock. Before Jim could respond, Julian shifted lower on the bed. He spread Jim's legs and knelt between them.

"Watch him take your dick into his mouth," Michael whispered.

As if Jim was going to miss this.

He grabbed a pillow, shoved it under his head, and shivered as Julian took his shaft in his warm hand and bent over it. That first flick of his tongue across the head of Jim's cock sent tremors rippling through him, and he gasped.

"Does that feel good?" Michael asked.

Jim rolled his eyes. "Do I really need to answer that?" Then he groaned as Julian took him deep. Jim pushed up with his hips, wanting more of that delicious wet heat, and Julian's head bobbed as he shifted into a higher gear. Michael's lips met Jim's, and Jim opened for him, caught between two glorious sensations as both men explored him with their tongues.

Everything came to a halt when Julian paused and stared at him as he slid gentle fingers over Jim's balls, past his taint, and finally brushed them over his hole. "God, that's beautiful."

No one had *ever* talked like that about Jim's body. A tingling sensation swept across his face.

Julian fell silent, maintaining eye contact, his fingertips tracing a slow circle around Jim's entrance.

Jim got the message. It had to come from him. He shivered. "Fuck me."

Michael kissed his neck. "Julian will be the first of us to be inside you."

The implication was all too clear. Michael would get his turn too. Then all such thoughts were swept away when Michael reached over to the nightstand, grabbed the bottle of lube that stood there, and tossed it to Julian.

Jim caught his breath, his heart pounding. "How… how do you want me?"

Julian smiled. "Patience, baby. Daddy has to do a little exploring first."

That one word sent a wave of heat crashing through him, and his breathing quickened.

Julian nodded slowly. "You like that, don't you?"

"It shows, huh?" Like was too mild a word. That word reached into Jim's innards and twisted them, making him hungry to hear it again.

"Oh, a little." Julian's eyes were bright with amusement. He opened the bottle and squeezed the viscous liquid onto his fingers.

"How did you know?" How could Julian have known what that single word would do to him? Like the other night. How had Julian known to be rough with his nipples?

A brief cloud crossed Julian's face, but then it was gone. "Let's call it a skill, okay? Now... spread a bit wider for me."

Jim did as instructed, his breath hitching when the coolness of the lube came into contact with his hole. Michael tightened his hold, pulling Jim closer. Their lips met as Julian leisurely sank his finger into Jim's body, and Jim moaned into the kiss.

A low cry tumbled from his lips when Julian found his prostate, and Jim jerked his head to stare at him.

Julian nodded. "How does that feel?"

"A-amazing." He wanted to howl in frustration when Julian withdrew his finger.

Julian grinned. "The kind of amazing that makes you want to spread your legs even wider for me? That wants me to get the fuck back inside you?"

"Yeah!" Beside him, Michael laughed softly.

Julian gave a satisfied smile. "Bingo." He slid his finger back into Jim, and crooked it. Jim's groan filled the air, and Julian's smile intensified. "That's where I need to go." Another deliberate stroke over Jim's gland. "You feel that? Imagine how it's going to feel when it's my dick in there, opening you up. Because that's what's coming next. It's going to make you feel so good."

Jim didn't doubt him for a second.

Julian added another finger, and Jim sighed. "Yes." Julian continued to tease his hole until he was squirming, desperate for more.

Then Julian grabbed Jim's hips and tugged him. "I want you with your ass over the edge." He got off the bed and stood at the foot of it, squeezing lube onto his shaft. Jim shifted lower, his heartbeat rapid, and Michael moved with him, kneeling at his head.

"Grab your legs, and bring your knees to your chest." Julian stroked his slick cock. When Jim did as he was told, Julian brought the head of his dick to Jim's hole, applying gentle pressure. Then he leaned over, slipping his arms under Jim's pits and cradling him, his face barely an inch from Jim's.

They locked gazes, and something fluttered in Jim's chest.

"All I need you to do?" Julian's eyes were warm. "Look at me, and relax." And as Jim expelled a long breath, Julian slowly slid his dick inside him with a sigh.

"Daddy's got you."

Chapter 11

Jim held his breath, and Michael stroked his cheek. "Breathe, baby. You have to relax. That makes it easier."

"Never... never felt so full," Jim gasped out. "Feels like my insides are hugging his cock."

Julian stilled inside him. He brushed his lips over Jim's ear. "I'm not all the way in, but I'm going to stay right here. When you want more, squeeze it. Okay?"

Jim managed a nod before Julian kissed him, an unhurried, tender kiss that was exactly what he needed. Jim let go of his legs and cupped Julian's face. "You can go a little deeper." He gave an experimental squeeze around Julian's dick, and Julian groaned.

"Oh, good boy."

The words of praise warmed Jim, and his chest swelled.

Julian glanced at Michael. "Jesus, it feels so good inside him. So fucking tight."

Michael caressed Jim's face. "You're going to be feeling both of us today."

"Just not at the same time, okay?" Jim joked. He stifled a groan of pleasure as Julian inched a little deeper.

Julian caught his chin and held him steady. "There's no one to hear you, sweetheart. You let it out, all right? If you want to fucking yell, you do it. It's just us, baby boy."

Jim swallowed and went with his gut. "Yes, Daddy."

Oh my God, the way he's looking at me…

"You beautiful boy." Julian buried his face in Jim's neck, kissing him there. "This dick is yours today, sweetheart. And once I touch that spot, you're going to want me deeper." He moved, the slightest of motions, and Jim caught his breath.

"Don't think I've ever felt a dick so deep in me."

Julian's eyes were warm as he locked gazes with Jim. "You've got two holes, right?" When Jim stared at him, Julian nodded. "You've got a second hole inside there, and it's tight. So we've got to loosen it up a little." He smiled. "We might not get there *this* time, but we will."

Heat surged through Jim. *This time.* Fuck, yeah.

"You ready?"

Before Jim could ask "Ready for what?" Julian pushed, and exquisite sensations bombarded him. "Fuck. Keep it there, keep it there." God, this was heaven.

Julian nodded, his hips rolling. "Daddy's got you."

"And this Daddy's got you too." Michael bent down to kiss him, and Jim responded with a hunger he hadn't known he possessed. A groan fell from his lips when Michael teased his nipples, and Michael sighed. "That's it, beautiful boy. Let it out." Then he straightened, his cock jutting out, hard and proud, and Jim *wanted*.

He craned his neck and sucked on the head, loving Michael's moan. Jim took him a little deeper until both his mouth and ass were full.

"Fuck, he's good at that." Michael grabbed Jim's head and rocked, sliding his dick in and out, and Jim couldn't get enough. He licked along Michael's length, flicking under the wide head with his tongue, then pushing it into his slit. "Holy fuck," Michael groaned. "Love your tongue, boy."

Julian hooked his arms under Jim's knees, his legs resting on Julian's shoulders, and settled into a leisurely rhythm that was goddamn perfect.

"That's it." Michael kissed Julian. "Nice and slow. Just stroke in and out of him." He gazed down at Jim, freeing his dick from Jim's mouth. "Does it feel good when he fucks you?"

"It feels fucking *awesome*," Jim blurted.

Michael bent over and kissed him. "I want to feel that talented tongue of yours in my ass."

Jim's circuits just about blew. "Yes," he breathed, tremors of anticipation trickling through him.

Michael straddled his head, facing Julian, and Jim got his first look at Michael's firm, hairy ass. He grabbed Michael's cheeks and spread him, stretching his hole, gazing at the furry cleft above him.

"Fuck yeah. Do it." Michael's voice shook. Jim flicked his tongue against that tantalizing hole, and a shudder rippled through Michael. "More." Jim licked and sucked, pushing against the muscle that loosened for him. "Now my balls," Michael demanded, shifting back. Jim took one of them into his mouth, and the loud moan that escaped Michael only made him want to drag more of them from Michael's lips. Michael and Julian kissed, each feeding the other soft noises that spoke of pleasure, and Jim had never felt so fucking *powerful*.

Then Michael moved, clambering off the bed. He grabbed the lube and slicked his cock, then moved to stand behind Julian. He leaned in and brought his lips to Julian's ear. "Keep fucking him while you ride my dick. Just sit on it."

Julian stilled, withdrawing a little as he inched back, and Jim knew the instant Michael was inside him. Julian's eyes widened, and his breath left him in short bursts. "Fucking *love* your cock."

"That's it. Show Jim what you look like when you take a dick."

Julian leaned over Jim once more, kissing him hungrily as Michael moved in and out of him, his hands tight on Julian's hips. Julian groaned, shuttling between them, and Jim's body was suddenly alight, his skin tingling.

Julian swallowed. "I can't hold back. I have to breed your ass."

Jim gaped at him. "Do it. Fucking *do* it." He wanted to feel Julian's warmth filling him. He grabbed Julian's shoulders, his fingers digging into the muscled flesh. "Breed me, Daddy." Every cell in his body zinged, and he shivered. He fucking *wanted* this, needed it like he needed air.

"Fuck yeah, breed him," Michael echoed.

Julian's eyes were huge. "Oh fuck." He stiffened, and Jim felt the tell-tale throb inside him. "Giving you my load," Julian gasped, his hips jerking. Their lips met, and Jim moaned into the kiss, not wanting it to end. He wrapped his arms around Julian, holding him against his chest, his heels resting on the swell of Julian's ass.

"So warm," Jim murmured. The knowledge that there was nothing between them was heady as fuck.

"The way you two look…" Michael kissed Julian's back. "My turn."

Julian gave Jim one last kiss before slowly pulling out of him. He lay beside Jim on the bed, stroking his damp body, and kissing his chest and nipples. "You are amazing," he whispered.

Michael moved closer, stroking Jim's ass. "Push out his cum. Do it. Push it out onto my dick." His chest glistened with sweat.

Jim bore down, expelling Julian's spunk, and Michael smeared it over his heavy, long cock. Julian tossed him the lube, and he squeezed some onto his fingers, then slid them into Jim's ass. Michael's eyes twinkled. "You can never have too much lube." He brought the head to Jim's hole, gazing down at it. "Fucking beautiful hole, all wide and ready for me." Then his eyes met Jim's as he pushed, and Jim groaned at the exquisite friction. Michael nodded, his face flushed. "That's it, boy. You just try to keep me out of there. Try to push me out. Because I'm not going anywhere. Right now, this is *my* hole."

Jim couldn't hold the words in. "Yes, Daddy." Then Michael bent him in half as Julian had done, slipping his arms under Jim's shoulders to cradle him, and Jim had never felt so cherished. They exchanged kisses, Julian joining in before Michael straightened, grasping Jim's ankles and spreading him wide. Julian got into a kneeling position next to Jim's head, and Jim turned to clean Julian's cock with his tongue, his body buffeted as Michael rocked in and out of him, no longer gentle but slamming into him.

Jim was on fire, the need to come white-hot.

"It's my turn to breed this beautiful ass." Michael tightened his grip on Jim's ankles, hips snapping as he drove his cock deep. Jim locked his gaze on Michael, his body tense, awaiting that heat within him.

Michael grabbed Jim's head, cradling it as he lifted it from the bed, and leaned over to claim his mouth in a passionate kiss. Their foreheads met, and Michael whispered, "Daddy's got you." Then he thrust deep, and Jim cried out as Michael shot hard inside him. They remained locked in that position, Michael's warmth filling him, Michael's dick buried in him to the hilt, Jim aware of Julian moving to sit behind him, his arms around Jim. His skin was slick, his hole stretched and aching, and his legs felt like jelly.

Jim had never been happier.

Michael kissed him, a sweet brushing of lips against his, and Julian leaned in to join them. "Your turn," Julian whispered. Then Michael eased his spent dick out of him, and bent over to take Jim's cock in his mouth while he slid a couple of fingers into Jim's loosened hole, releasing a slow trickle of cum. Jim shuddered as Michael stroked his gland, and seconds later he pulsed spunk into Michael's mouth, shaking with every throb of his dick until he was done.

Michael licked his lips. "Delicious." He got onto the bed, and Jim found himself sandwiched between two warm men, who held him, stroked and caressed him, and kissed him, their legs intertwined, their arms around one another.

A sense of loss overwhelmed him, so acute that his chest ached from it.

Michael drew Jim to him. "Still with us?" He kissed Jim's forehead, and the tender gesture made him ache even more.

Jim swallowed. "You... you said I had an open invitation to come over here whenever I liked. That I didn't need to wait to be asked." His heartbeat quickened. "Does that offer extend to your bed?" Michael glanced at Julian, and Jim's heart sank. "I'm sorry. I keep forgetting, you both have work."

Julian stopped his words with a kiss. "The answer is yes. For as long as you're staying here."

That brought a dash of cold reality. This working break was a fragile bubble of time, and the day would come when it would shatter, and Jim would go back to San Francisco.

Don't think about that now. Enjoy it while it lasts.

A whine came from below, and Michael chuckled. "Oh dear. Someone's not happy."

"A treat will soon cure that," Julian said confidently. "So how about we grab a shower, and then I'll make us lunch." He grinned. "My, the morning went fast."

"You'll stay for lunch?" Michael inquired.

Jim nodded. "I'd love to." He wanted to spend as much time with them as they would allow.

Michael beamed. "And then afterward, I'd like you to come into my studio. I've had an epiphany, and I need you to help me realize it."

"Me?"

Michael laughed. "Yes, you. Right now I feel inspired." His stomach grumbled, and he gave them a sheepish glance. "I also feel hungry. Can't think why that should be." His eyes glittered.

Julian got off the bed. "Come on. It's a walk-in shower, and there's plenty of room for three." His lips twitched. "Come to think of it, we've had more than three in there, but that was Michael's fiftieth birthday party, and—"

Michael cleared his throat. "I'm sure Jim doesn't want to hear about *that*."

Jim laughed, suffused with a lightness that banished all thoughts of what was to come. There seemed little point in dwelling on his departure. He wanted to enjoy his time with them.

And besides, he was about to encounter another first, and the prospect of the three of them under jets of hot water obviously appealed to part of his anatomy.

Julian chuckled. "I was going to lead you by the *hand* to the shower, but now I'm having other ideas."

Michael coughed. "Save the shenanigans for later. Shower sex is for younger men than you and I."

Julian grinned. "Exactly. And Jim here is the younger man." He gave Jim an impish glance. "And *this* Daddy wants to play with our boy's dick."

Jim stilled at his words, and Michael kissed his shoulder. "While you're here…"

He nodded, understanding instantly. "While I'm here," he repeated. For the rest of his stay, Jim was to be their boy.

Jim didn't question how Julian saw so much, or his own reactions. He only knew that calling them Daddy in the heat of such glorious sex had been the right thing to do. He *felt* it, balls to bones. It wasn't something he'd ever fantasized about, or wished for, but as soon as the word had been uttered, as soon as it was out there in the ether, he'd known.

Is that what's been missing all this time? Is this what I needed?

Jim didn't have a clue. He just knew he wanted more.

Chapter 12

"You're sure you're okay about this?" Michael asked as they walked to his studio.

Jim laughed. "Well, that depends on what *this* is. If you're asking am I okay spending more time here, then yes, absolutely. If you're asking am I okay with whatever you have planned, then I have no clue, because you haven't seen fit to share that part with me." He'd had a great day so far. Of course, he had aches where there hadn't been any for a long time, but each one was a delicious reminder of his morning in their bed. Jim's head was still spinning. The change in them during sex...

Was I seeing them as they truly are? He'd known they were two sensual men, but *holy fuck*, the things they'd said... And as for being their *boy* for the duration of his stay, Jim had no issue with that whatsoever. He shivered at the recollection of those three little words that had sent both heat and ice flushing through him in equal measure.

'Daddy's got you.'

"Jim?"

He gave a start. They were standing in front of Michael's studio, and Michael was staring at him with obvious amusement. "Sorry." Jim smiled. "My mind was someplace else."

Michael's eyes gleamed. "I don't think I need three

guesses to know where." He pushed the door open, and Jim followed him inside. The first thing Michael did was to switch on the space heaters that stood at intervals on the floor. Jim wandered over to the six-foot-high chunk of wood and stroked it. There was something so sensual about wood that invited touch.

"Have you given any more thought to what you're going to do with this?"

Michael coughed. "Actually? Yes. That's why I've brought you here." He came over to Jim and gazed at the wood. "Remember I said I wanted to carve a male nude? Well… I was wondering…"

Jim froze as he put two and two together. "Me? You want to carve *me*?"

Michael nodded. "Seeing you in the flesh, as it were, was inspirational."

Jim's chest swelled. "Oh. Wow."

"You *can* say no, okay?" Michael swallowed.

Fuck that. Jim loved the idea. "What do you need me to do?"

"Seriously?" Michael's face lit up, and seeing his happiness send warmth flooding through Jim. "Okay, I'd need to take photos and do some sketches."

Jim pointed to the three space heaters. "Only if they form a circle around me. Otherwise, I can see my nipples freezing and dropping off, and something else retracting completely."

Michael laughed. "Deal." He went over to a chest, pulled open the top drawer, and removed several sheets of white paper.

Jim smiled to himself. Michael was already lost to his task. Jim moved the space heaters into position, and then proceeded to stand in the middle as he stripped off. "Do you want me standing, sitting, lying down…?"

Michael grabbed a stool and brought it into the warm space. "You can sit on this. You might be here for a while." He looked Jim in the eye. "You're sure about this?"

Impulsively, Jim kissed him on the mouth. "I'm sure." Michael's eyes widened at the gesture, and Jim stilled. "Are you... allowed to kiss me if Julian's not here?"

Michael bit his lip. "Technically? No. But I see nothing wrong in sharing a chaste kiss." He leaned in and pressed his lips to Jim's cheek, and its sweetness gave Jim a major case of the warm fuzzies. "I think you'd better take off your own jeans. That might prove more temptation than I can stand." He bit back a grin before retreating beyond the circle of heaters to where he'd set up an easel.

Jim removed his jeans and stood naked in the middle of Michael's studio. Despite the warmth, he shivered, but he lifted his chin high and pushed his shoulder back. "I'm ready."

Michael gazed at him with gleaming eyes. "And you're beautiful."

He spent five or so minutes arranging Jim on the stool: one leg like *so*, one arm *here*, the other *here*... When Michael was ready, he picked up a pencil and smiled. "Let's begin."

"Is it okay if we talk while you sketch, or do you not multitask?"

Michael chuckled. "I can talk and draw at the same time. And yes, let's talk."

Jim knew exactly what he wanted to discuss. That look in Julian's eyes earlier...

"When we were upstairs, and Julian was playing with my nipples... I asked him how he'd known to be rough with them, and he said it was a skill. But…"

Michael paused, his pencil in mid-air. "But?"

"It was his expression. It was almost as if something painful had flashed through his head. I may have imagined it, I suppose." One glance at Michael's face, however, told him otherwise. "Forget I asked. That's none of my business." Michael went back to his drawing. Jim's mind went back to their bedroom. "Can I ask you something a little personal?"

"You can *ask*."

Jim took a deep breath. "How many 'boys' have there been? Because I'm guessing there have been quite a few."

Michael put down his pencil and stepped away from the easel. "There were a lot of boys when we lived in LA. We used to go to a certain club. I supposed you could call it a Daddies club. Guys who went in for older men, Daddies looking for a boy, boys looking for a Daddy… all permutations. There was nothing heavy. We kept things casual, and to be honest, it was just about the sex, like it was for most of the guys who frequented the place. Needs were met, so to speak."

Jim stared at him. "I never realized such places existed."

Michael smiled. "That doesn't surprise me. We loved going there on the weekend. More often than not, there'd be a boy in our beds Saturday night, and by Sunday night he'd be gone." His face tightened. "That was before…"

Hair prickled on the back of Jim's neck. "What happened?"

Michael sighed. "We met someone. Kristofer. You could call him the boy who stayed."

"What was so different about him, compared to

the others?"

"He was a newbie." Michael's eyes shone. "We exposed him to a whole new world, and he loved it. Every time was... an unforgettable experience." He swallowed. "Julian and I, we swore we'd keep things light, just like we had with the boys before him, but..." His gaze met Jim's. "We fell for him," Michael said simply. "We had an open relationship. We told Kristofer he wasn't ours exclusively... though we wanted him to be. So we left the cage door open, and our beautiful bird flew in and out, content with the way things were."

Jim's heart sank. "What went wrong?" It was obvious *something* had.

Michael's shoulders drooped and he stared off into the distance. "He met someone. That wasn't the problem, though. We were happy for him, because *one look* told us how much in love he was with this guy, Ray. Then came the day when he told Ray about us."

Jim's throat tightened. "I think I can guess the rest."

Michael nodded. "Kristofer came to see us one night. He said Ray had given him an ultimatum—monogamy or nothing. He didn't like the idea of Kristofer having two Daddies." A spasm contorted Michael's face. "What could we do? Kristofer fucking *loved* him. So... we decided on a clean break. We promised we'd stay out of his life, we wouldn't seek him out..."

"And did you?"

Another slow nod. "We kept our word. Oh, we saw him again—always at a distance, of course—and God, that hurt." His eyes darkened. "It broke Julian. I couldn't bear to see him like that."

"But you were hurting too." He still was, Jim could see that.

"Not long after, we made the move here."

"Just like that? Why here?"

Michael sighed once more. "It wasn't a spur-of-the-moment decision, a reaction to Kristofer's departure. We'd been discussing a move for a while. We used to take vacations in national parks, looking for someplace where we felt we could be happy, but the timing was never right. Maybe Kristofer leaving us was the kick in the pants we both needed. We took a trip to Yosemite that summer, and found this place. That was it. End of search."

"Did you ever hear from Kristofer again?"

"No. To be honest, it's been years since we thought about him." He locked gazes with Jim. "*You* brought him back."

"Me?"

Michael gave a warm smile. "You're so like him. Your reactions… Julian noticed it first."

Something clicked into place. "I *didn't* imagine that look, did I? I reminded Julian of Kristofer."

"Yes. But you're not Kristofer. You're *you*." He went back to the easel and picked up his pencil, and Jim resumed his original position.

"You and Julian… you're so different in bed."

"In what way?"

A shiver rippled through Jim. "I think it's the way you talk, mostly. It's nothing like how you are normally."

Michael peered around the easel. "And how *are* we 'normally'?"

"Quiet, cultured… You when you're fucking? That's a whole different animal."

"But did you like it?"

Jim laughed. "If I said yes, that would be the understatement of the year. I've never met anyone who talked so... dirty in bed, but I loved it."

There it was again. *'Daddy's got you.'*

Jim didn't understand his visceral reaction to their words. He was *thirty-six years old,* for Christ's sake. Calling *anyone* Daddy at his age had to be wrong, but Lord help him, it had felt so right.

"Christmas is next week."

Jim blinked. "Excuse me?"

Michael stared at him. "Christmas. You know, Santa and Frosty? Presents? Ham? Christmas tree? Granted, we haven't put ours up yet—that will be done this week. But my point is, you'll be here for Christmas. And you are *not* spending it alone in that cabin." His eyes sparkled. "Spend it with us."

Jim hadn't given Christmas a thought. It wasn't as if he celebrated it. There was just him. His parents had made the move to Florida a decade ago, but even so, they didn't want him around, not with his 'perverted ways', and quite frankly, he didn't want to be around them. Christmas was spent at home, avoiding crowds, and writing.

"Let me persuade you," Michael said with a grin. "Plenty of food, a roaring fire, music, cuddles on the couch, Buster..."

Jim laughed. "There you go. Buster was the deciding factor." Not that he needed much persuasion. The prospect of spending the holiday with Michael and Julian gave him a fluttery feeling in his belly and sent tingles all over him. Then he remembered. "Okay, but... I need to get some serious words done before then."

Michael beamed. "Are you feeling inspired too?"

He shrugged. "Just something I want to try." He'd made plenty of notes—now it was time to see if he could pull them all together into some kind of narrative.

"Okay. The offer stands." Michael's eyes twinkled. "Julian and I will be your reward for getting the words down. But… don't sleep alone, okay? Not when we have a big bed with a Jim-shaped space in it."

Oh God. The thought of sleeping with them, their arms wrapped around one another, the intimacy…

Plus the sex. Don't forget the sex. Because Jim had a feeling there would be a *lot* of that.

"I would love to spend my nights with you."

Michael put down his pencil, walked over to where Jim sat on the stool, and gave him another chaste kiss. "I'm so glad," he whispered. He glanced down to where Jim's dick jerked. "Something *else* seem happy about it too. In fact…" He retreated back to the easel. "Whatever you're thinking, keep thinking it. I want to finish my sketch."

Jim laughed. "You mean, you want to draw me with a hard-on. Why? Surely you can't carve me like that? Who would want to buy it?"

Michael chuckled. "Who says I'm going to sell it? Now sit still and think about what we're going to do with you after dinner."

Jim's heart pounded, and his cock rose.

"Oh, that's perfect. And I know just what Julian will want to do with that."

Jim had a feeling he knew too.

Chapter 13

"Is it straight?"

Michael glanced up at the Christmas tree and grinned. "About as straight as you or I. Want to let me at it now?" They had this argument every Christmas Eve. Julian would insist on setting the tree in its stand, and then Michael would take over to put it right.

Julian huffed. "Fine. You do that. *I'll* plug in the lights to make sure they all work." He reached into one of the numerous plastic boxes that contained their Christmas decorations, and withdrew a huge tangle of green cable and tiny clear lights.

Michael sighed. "I think it's time to retire them."

Julian jerked his head in Michael's direction. "What? No way. They work just great."

Michael reached into the box, took out a small plastic bag, and held it up in front of Julian's face. "You're running out of spare bulbs. And when you finally use the last one, you won't be able to buy more. *No one* makes lights like this anymore. They're all LED lights now. No push-in bulbs. No filaments to break." He grinned. "No more examining every single light, trying to find the one bulb that's blown."

"But… we've had these for—"

"Forever." Michael looked into Julian's eyes. "So maybe it's time for a change."

Julian stared at him, his Adam's apple bobbing. Finally his shoulders sagged. "You're right. After

Christmas, we'll go shopping for more, so we're ready for next year. Can we have one last time with them?"

Michael kissed him slowly on the lips. "One last time," he said as he drew back. "Go on. Plug them in. Let's see if they still work."

Julian chuckled as he unwound the plug. "I still think it's witchcraft. They work perfectly well when you take them down in January every year, but somehow between then and December, gremlins get in." He pushed the plug into the outlet and hundreds of white lights winked into existence. Julian gaped. "I don't fucking believe it. That hasn't happened in years." He gave Michael a hopeful glance. "Hey, does this mean—"

"No, it does *not*," Michael replied firmly. "We are still changing them. Now let me straighten up this tree, and then we can get on with the job of decorating it before Jim gets here." He wanted everything ready for when Jim joined them that afternoon. Michael couldn't wait to see his face.

"I like this routine we've gotten into," Julian murmured as he held the tree steady while Michael unscrewed the bolts that captured it in the stand.

"What routine are you talking about?" Michael got up and walked a distance away from the tree, casting a critical eye over it. "A little to the left?" Julian did as instructed. "A bit more. Stop there. Don't move." He crouched at the foot of the tree and quickly screwed the bolts into position.

"This past week. Jim comes to dinner, he stays the night, we have breakfast together the next morning, he leaves to go write, we go do our thing, and then by evening he's back again." Julian's eyes glittered. "Not that the nights are routine."

Michael had to agree with him. Jim had blossomed before their eyes, responding to suggestions with increasing enthusiasm, displaying a boldness that was both exciting and unexpected.

"All I can say is, we must have been very good Daddies this year, for Santa to bring us such a gift." Julian let out a happy sigh. "It's been wonderful having him in our bed."

"You mean, in our lives." Michael stood and took the tangle of wire from Julian's hands.

"Aren't they the same thing?"

Michael took in Julian's sparkling eyes and his flushed neck and cheeks. "Don't."

Julian blinked. "Don't what?" That single bob of his Adam's apple said a lot.

Michael placed the lights on the couch, then put his hands on Julian's shoulders. "I know you. I know the signs. Don't lose your heart."

Julian's mouth fell open. "Damn. You really *do* see right through me, don't you?"

Michael couldn't let him labor under any illusions. "Does it occur to you that I know how you're feeling because I recognize those same emotions in myself?"

Those warm brown eyes widened. "Then you—"

Michael pressed a single finger to Julian's lips. "I won't let us go through that again. The last time hurt too much. So for *both* our sakes, we need to remember one thing—when the rental is up, Jim will go. How big a hole he leaves in our life here will depend on how much we let him in."

Julian gaped at him. "'*Let* him in'? Christ, he's already through the door. He has a toothbrush in our bathroom, for God's sake." Then he crumpled before Michael's eyes, leaning into him, making Michael aware of the shivers that coursed through him.

"Hey," Michael said softly, holding him.

Julian buried his face in Michael's neck. "We don't have long left with him."

Michael stroked his back. "Then we make the most of every minute, okay?" He lifted Julian's chin with his fingers. "And we try not to fall in love with him."

"You mean, more than we already have done?" Julian's eyes glistened.

Michael had no words for him. Julian had nailed it.

He gave Julian another kiss. "Come on. We've got a lot of work to do if we're going to be ready for Jim." He smiled. "He won't recognize the place when we're done with it."

Keeping busy also meant keeping his mind from thoughts that tormented him.

By the sound of it, thoughts that tormented both of them.

Jim closed the laptop with a contented sigh. *How long has it been since words have flown like this?* Long enough that the experience excited him beyond measure. It wasn't that he hadn't loved writing the murder mysteries series, but *this*? This was new and shiny. Each morning as he walked back to the cabin, his head was awash with ideas, scenarios, conversations... His characters never shut up, and Jim freaking *loved* that. Once he'd finished the first chapter, the compulsion to write more overtook him, and in one week he'd written forty-five thousand words. He'd gotten used to three to four thousand words a day before this, but this fervor wouldn't abate. He made every minute spent at the laptop count, and each evening when he finished for the day, it was with profound satisfaction. Jim had made a promise to himself: if he wanted a night with Michael and Julian, he had to damn well *earn* it.

Except tonight was Christmas Eve, and Jim knew he'd get no writing done the following day, but that was okay. The end was in sight. If this heady rush continued, he'd be leaving in early January with a book ready to be sent to—

To whom? His publisher? Was he going to publish it traditionally, or dip his toes into the hitherto unknown waters of self-publishing?

Jim hadn't gotten as far as a decision about the book's destiny. And there was no way he was going to think about it that night, not when two gorgeous bears awaited him.

Does that make me a cub? The thought tickled him. Then heat spread throughout his body. *I'm their boy—for another two weeks or so.* Two more weeks of waking up sandwiched between them, their hands reaching over him as if somehow in their sleep, they'd needed to connect the three of them. Two more weeks of glorious sex that had rocked his world. Two more weeks of sitting on their couch, posing in Michael's studio, watching Julian paint…

That last had been the shocker. If Michael's expression had been anything to go by, Julian did *not* admit spectators, and yet he'd issued the invitation. Jim had sat on the red velvet couch, watching every stroke of Julian's brushes on the canvas, not daring to utter a word, but grateful to be there.

It was amazing how well he'd come to know them in such a short time. Michael was the rock, Julian's anchor. It was his calm that pervaded their home, a calm Jim drank in eagerly. Trying to keep up with Julian as his mind flitted from topic to topic with little or no warning, was becoming a daily task that Jim relished. The best part? The closeness he'd observed between them, the sensuality, the intimacy... All those things had been extended to include Jim, and each day brought new depths to the emotions that were only now surfacing for the first time in Jim's memory.

I ran away from these things. And yet they were the inspiration breathing life into his new book. For the first time he was writing about sexual intimacy, every word brought to life by his experiences. And he knew if he let Michael or Julian anywhere near his precious manuscript, they'd see themselves instantly in his characters Mike and Jake.

There are two men waiting for you. You're wasting valuable kissing time. God knew, Jim loved how much they kissed. And more often than not, what started out as kissing on the couch led to the bedroom.

He couldn't get enough of them.

The knock at the door made his heart beat faster. "Ho ho ho?"

Jim dashed over to the door with a grin, and opened it to find Michael on the doormat, bundled up in his usual thick jacket, but wearing a bright red Santa hat with white fur trim. A soft-looking red scarf adorned his neck.

"I'm not late, am I?" Jim asked. "I said I'd be there by five, and it's only four-thirty."

Michael stepped into the cabin and closed the door

behind him. "No, you're not late. I just got impatient, that's all. We're waiting for you so we can start celebrating Christmas."

Warmth flooded him. "Aw. That's sweet." He glanced at the floor. "You didn't bring Buster?"

Michael chuckled. "Buster is in his cozy bed, chewing on his new toy. And waiting for you to come cuddle him." He took a step toward Jim. "Which was exactly what *I* was waiting for too."

Jim's heartbeat quickened, and all he wanted in that moment was for Michael to kiss him.

That's against the rules, remember?

"Let me grab a change of clothes for tomorrow." He went over to the drawers where he kept his sweaters and underwear.

"You could always go commando."

Jim jerked his head around to find Michael giving him a wicked smile. "Excuse me?"

Michael pointed to the white briefs in Jim's hand. "Leave them. It would give me a thrill, knowing you're bare beneath that zipper." His eyes gleamed. "Fewer layers to remove."

Jim swallowed. "You have a one-track mind, do you know that?" Not that he was complaining. When it came to sex, Michael's mind was deliciously inventive.

Michael held up his gloved hands. "Your choice. I've said my piece."

Jim glanced at the briefs. *Fuck it.* He placed them back into the drawer, not looking in Michael's direction. He didn't have to—Michael's soft chuckle said plenty. His bag packed, Jim gave the cabin a final glance. *Damn it.*

"What's wrong?"

Jim sighed. "Was I that obvious?"

Michael shrugged. "I just got the feeling you were unhappy about something."

Jim nodded. "I don't have gifts for you and Julian." He hadn't even thought about such a thing until that morning.

Michael came over to him and enfolded Jim in his strong arms. "Having you share Christmas with us is the best gift you could possibly give. So please, don't think like that. How long have we got you for?"

"Until the twenty-seventh?" Jim could afford to spend two days away from his laptop, given how much he'd already accomplished.

Michael beamed. "Perfect. Then let's get out of here. Julian has mulled wine waiting for you." His lips were inches from Jim's, his breath warm and smelling of chocolate and spiced rum. And *fuck*, Jim wanted those lips on his.

"Mulled wine sounds great," he murmured. He closed the gap a little more, and Michael's eyes widened.

It was Michael's turn to swallow. "We'd better go." He pulled back, releasing Jim, then grabbed Jim's bag. "Allow me. Get your coat on."

By the time they stepped out into the crisp air, Jim's heartbeat had returned to its normal rhythm. The crunch of newly fallen snow beneath their feet was the only sound apart from the chirrup of birds. The sun was setting, and Jim couldn't wait to see their house, lit up from within.

"Can I help with dinner?" Even as Jim asked the question, he knew what the response would be. Julian ruled the kitchen.

"Dinner is already taken care of. We don't have a cooked meal on Christmas Eve. Instead, we kind of graze. There's cheese of all descriptions, pâté, crackers, whatever we take a fancy to."

"Sounds like a carpet picnic." Jim had loved that phrase ever since he heard it in *Pretty Woman*.

"Exactly!" Michael caught his arm. "Do you trust me?"

"Yes." Jim didn't have to think about it.

"Okay." Michael removed his scarf and placed it over Jim's eyes. "I'll guide you. I just want something to be a surprise, that's all."

Jim's heart raced again. "Okay." Michael's gloved hand took his, and he walked with care, following Michael's instructions as they made their way along the lane.

Michael brought him to a halt, and turned him. "Ready?"

"Sure." The scarf removed, Jim caught his breath at the sight before him. The inside of the house seemed ablaze with lights. The Christmas tree was covered in them, and they adorned every window frame. The fir trees bracketing the house were festooned with lights too. "You got all this done since I left this morning? Wow. You must have worked like Trojans." He followed Michael to the side porch, where Buster already had his paws up on the glass door, his tail wagging.

"Someone's happy to see you," Michael observed.

As soon as Jim opened the door, Buster was dancing around his ankles with great exuberance, jumping up with little whines. Jim scooped him into his arms, and Buster licked his ear. "Thank you, Buster. And Merry Christmas to you too." The excitement had obviously gotten to the little dog—he wriggled in Jim's arms but made no attempt to get down. Jim noted the new collar around his neck. "I see Santa has already been here."

Michael laughed. "Delayed gratification is not in Buster's vocabulary. Besides, he has more presents for tomorrow." He grinned. "Yes, we spoil our dog. Bite me."

Jim deposited the wriggling Buster onto his bed. "Hey, you're his daddies. You do what you like." As he straightened, Michael grasped Jim's coat and held it for him as Jim freed his arms.

"You're here at last." Julian came into the living room, his arms wide. "God, it feels like I haven't seen you for *hours*." His eyes twinkled.

Before Jim could greet him, Michael put Jim's coat on the couch, and Jim found himself surrounded by strong arms. "Now I can say hello properly," Michael said in a low voice. His lips were the first to take Jim's in a hungry kiss, and Jim responded with equal yearning. Then it was Julian's turn, and Jim gave himself up to the need that devoured him.

Julian broke the kiss. "Do you want a drink? Something to eat? Or—"

"Or. I'll go with 'or'."

The hitch in Julian's breathing was gratifying. "Bedroom?"

Jim glanced at the thick rug in front of the stove. "How about here?" His heart beat wildly.

Michael caught his breath. "Are you sure?"

Jim nodded. He figured passers-by were highly unlikely. Besides, the idea of being seen added a frisson of delicious wickedness never before encountered. He shivered. "All I want for Christmas is… the three of us, naked, in front of the fire."

Julian swallowed, then made a dash for the stairs.

Jim stared after him. "Something I said?"

Michael's breath tickled his ear. "He's gone to fetch the lube."

Jim feigned amazement. "You don't have some down here?" He had visions of lube secreted around the house in every nook and cranny.

Michael's sheepish expression was adorable. "We ran out a few weeks ago. I'd been meaning to replace it." He knelt on the rug, tugging Jim down with him. Moments later, Julian was there too.

Michael leaned in and kissed Jim on the mouth. "Time to unwrap our present."

Julian's lips teased Jim's neck. "Poor old Christmas. It only gets to come once a year. Whereas *you*…"

Michael kissed the other side of his neck. "You get to come until you have nothing left."

Jim put his arms around them. "I can't think of a better way to start the celebrations."

It promised to be the best—and most exhausting—Christmas ever.

Chapter 14

Jim opened his eyes and smiled. It didn't matter that he'd woken in their bed every morning for a week and a half—the happiness he experienced when he slowly emerged from sleep to find himself between them, had not diminished in the slightest. As far as this situation was concerned, familiarity did *not* breed contempt. In fact, each day brought something new—a demand he'd never made before, words from them that seemed to settle into his heart with a rightness that shocked him into silence, or a newfound pride in the delight he encountered in their company.

The year would end in a manner Jim couldn't have foreseen twelve months ago, or even a *month* ago.

Will things be different when I'm back in San Francisco? Will I be different?

Stupid question. He already was. But as to if he was ready to change the way he lived, Jim was on shakier ground. He remembered being on vacation with his family as a child. The feel of those two or three weeks, so totally disconnected from real life in some way, had made it all the more difficult when it came time to pack up and go back to reality. He recalled asking his mom why they couldn't just stay there forever.

As an adult, he knew the truth. *You can't hold Heaven in your hand forever. You have to let it go, trusting it will be there again when you most need it.*

"Good morning." Julian's murmur brought him

back to reality, then his warm hand on Jim's erect dick told him the direction his morning was about to take.

Another slice of heaven awaited him.

"Morning." Jim lay facing Julian, Michael curled around Jim's back, his arm draped protectively across Jim's waist. What surprised Jim was how they always kept him between them, surrounding him, enveloping him with their warmth.

He chuckled when Julian gave a slow tug on his cock. "Something you want?"

Julian's eyes were suddenly more alert. "I think I've waited long enough." He tightened his grip on Jim's shaft. "I want to ride you."

Jim's heartbeat raced, and he shrugged off the last remnants of slumber, feeling ultra-awake. So far, he hadn't topped, not that he'd minded in the least. It wasn't the first time Julian had made mention of taking Jim's dick, but that was as far as they'd gotten. The prospect of sliding into Julian's ass sent yet more blood heading south.

"No kiss?" he teased. "No foreplay?" Saying the words made him giddy. He'd never dreamed he could be so... at ease, so comfortable in his own skin—so bold.

"We can kiss while you're inside me."

Michael's wry chuckle announced his entry into the proceedings. "Just go with it. When Julian wakes up horny, that's all you can do."

Jim laughed. "But he wakes up horny every day."

Michael shifted, easing Jim onto his back. His eyes gleamed as he leaned over to kiss Jim. "And your point is?"

"Hey, can we get back to *this* point?" Julian demanded, still with his hand around the base of Jim's cock.

Both Jim and Michael laughed at that. "Will you do the honors?" Jim asked Michael, who immediately grabbed the bottle of lube from the nightstand. He squeezed a liberal amount onto Jim's solid shaft, and slicked up its length. Julian lost no time in straddling Jim, reaching behind him to guide its head between his ass cheeks. He gazed at Jim, his eyes bright, his pupils so dark…

"Ready to fuck Daddy?"

Jim's only response was to tilt his hips and *push*, gasping at the sensation as the head breached Julian's tight entrance. Julian nodded, his breathing shallow as he sank down, not stopping until Jim was all the way inside him. Julian swallowed. "Fuck. You're so deep." He leaned over and kissed Jim on the lips, his hand wrapped around his dick.

Jim rested his hands on Julian's hips, rocking up into him, shocked into silence by the exquisite feel of Julian's body as it sheathed his cock. When Julian sat up and began to ride, hips rolling fluidly, Jim let him do the work, feasting his eyes on the sight of Julian in motion, his body undulating, perspiration already coating his chest. "You look amazing," he told Julian. "Feels so good inside you." Better, in fact, than he ever remembered it being, way back before celibacy had become more appealing than the entanglement of emotions that always accompanied sex.

Michael knelt at Jim's head, turning it gently to take his dick. "Want to feel our boy's mouth on my cock."

Jim sucked it eagerly, not bothering to mute his moans around Michael's heavy shaft. Michael shifted once more to straddle Jim's chest, fucking his mouth with long, even strokes.

"Love your mouth," Michael murmured before he pulled free and bent down to kiss him. Michael's smile lit up his eyes. "Love your hole just as much."

Then he moved, and Jim groaned as Michael knelt behind Julian, knowing what was coming.

"Pass me a pillow?" Michael asked Julian, who grabbed one and passed it back. Michael shoved it under Jim's ass, and Julian leaned forward, his chest meeting Jim's.

"You won't be able to decide what you want to do—fuck me, or fuck yourself on his dick." Julian grinned. "Spoiled for choice."

Michael gripped Jim's thighs as he spread him. The *snick* of the lube bottle, slick fingers over Jim's hole, and *finally*... That first unhurried penetration pushed a sigh from Jim's lips.

Yes. Fuck, yes.

It didn't matter what they did in bed—*nothing* came close to how glorious it felt to be connected to both of them like this.

"It feels right, doesn't it?"

Jim caught his breath to hear Michael echo his own thoughts. "Yes." On top of him, Julian nodded, rolling his hips sensuously as he fucked himself on Jim's shaft.

Michael drove his cock all the way home. "It feels like it belongs there, doesn't it?"

"Fuck yes." The words fell from Jim's lips. He groaned when Michael withdrew. "Put it back in me." When there was no immediate response, Jim lifted his head from the pillow and gazed at Michael's face, visible over Julian. "Please, Daddy." Then he let out a low moan as Michael pushed back inside him.

There it was again, that sense of connection Jim craved, as addictive as a drug. And he knew exactly how he wanted it administered.

"Please, Daddy, go slow." He swallowed, shaking. "Make love to me."

Michael froze, and for an instant Jim feared he'd said too much. Julian's breathing hitched, and he raised himself up, Jim's cock falling to his belly with a wet *smack*. He lay beside Jim, sliding his arm beneath Jim's neck as he kissed Jim. Julian gazed at Michael. "Want to watch you make love to our boy."

Michael nodded, hooking his arms under Jim's knees. He slowly filled Jim to the hilt and paused, his face over Jim's. "Are you our boy?"

"Yes, Daddy." Jim's heart pounded.

Michael got into a rhythm that was goddamn perfect. "Is that what you need?"

"Yes, Daddy."

"Is this how you wanted it?"

"Oh, fuck yes, Daddy." Jim hadn't known it until that moment. Julian kissed him, his hands warm on Jim's dick, giving it leisurely tugs in time with Michael's thrusts. Then Michael's lips were on Jim's, and Julian's too, and there had never been a sweeter kiss.

Michael's sigh filled the air. "My men." Another kiss, another connection, and all the while Michael stroked his dick in and out of Jim, and Julian played with Jim's cock.

"Want me to ride you again?" Julian asked.

Jim couldn't hold the words in any longer. "Yes. That's the best thing, when it's all of us."

Michael flashed Julian a glance, then lifted Jim up off the mattress. For a moment, he slipped free of Jim's body as he lay on his back. "Ride *me*, sweetheart?"

Jim sat astride Michael's hips and guided Michael's dick back to where it belonged. Julian stroked Jim's back and shoulders, kissing him there.

Michael cupped Jim's face. "Want our loads in there?"

Elation filled him. "You have to ask?" Jim loved it when their dicks throbbed inside him, their warmth filling him.

Michael's soft kiss grazed his lips. "How would you like to feel Julian's cock in there, alongside mine?"

He stilled, unable to breathe.

"It's okay if you don't want that," Michael assured him.

Jim gaped at him, his mind racing. *What if it hurts?* Then just as quickly another thought followed it. *What if it's even more amazing than everything I've done so far? What if it* deepens *my connection with them?*

Oh God, he wanted that.

Jim took a breath. "The idea scares me but... I want to try."

Michael's face glowed. "That's our boy." His words lit a fire inside Jim, and warmth radiated throughout his body. Michael pulled Jim down to lie on Michael's chest, wrapping his arms around Jim. "Just relax. Breathe. Hold onto me. Daddy's got you."

Julian kissed down Jim's spine, and then Jim heard the telltale *click* of the lube bottle. Jim gave a shaky laugh. "You can never have too much lube, right?" He gasped as the slippery head of Julian's cock slid through his crack to where Michael already stretched him.

"Think how good it's going to feel when we're both making love to you," Julian said quietly.

God, yes. He *so* wanted to know how that felt. Then there was pressure, and Jim groaned. "Jesus."

"Sit down on it," Michael urged him. "That's it, just sit down on it, and breathe."

"Holy *fuck*." That feeling of being stretched had swelled into something *huge*, something that threatened to overwhelm him.

"Take a deep breath. Look into my eyes." Michael locked gazes with him. "We're both inside you."

"You're both so *big*," Jim gasped.

"And we're not going to move until you say so," Julian assured him. He stroked Jim's back, snaking a hand around Jim's waist to envelop his dick. "Relax, baby. Deep breaths. You've got us both."

"You're inside me?" Jim panted, trying to breathe through it.

"Don't panic, your Daddies have you." Michael's voice was soothing. "Did you ever dream you could do this?" He cupped Jim's nape with both hands, never breaking eye contact.

"Never," Jim burst out.

"It feels full, doesn't it?" Julian had one hand on Jim's cock and the other on his nipple. "I've been where you are, and I can't describe how my first time made me feel."

Neither could Jim. So many sensations intertwined. Yes, there was pain, but that soon morphed into discomfort, and then finally into something that he couldn't put into words.

Tears welled up and spilled onto Jim's cheeks, and Michael widened his eyes. "You want us to stop?"

Jim shook his head. "I don't know why I'm crying like this." That initial burn was fading, but the feeling of being so goddamn *full* hadn't abated. And yet he felt so freaking *light*. If Michael were to let go of him, Jim thought he might float off, swept away on the ever-increasing waves of pleasure that were already lapping at his feet.

Then he looked into Michael's eyes, and saw the same tears. *He feels it too.*

Jim shuddered out a long breath and kissed Michael's lips. "You can move now." Then all thoughts were washed away as Julian began to move, tiny increments at first but gaining in depth, his breath warm against Jim's ear. Michael held still, his hands still cradling Jim's head, his gaze fixed on Jim with a focus that left Jim in no doubt that this was more than anything they'd done before, that it *meant* something.

Julian let out a guttural moan. "Fuck, I'm gonna come."

That unmistakable warmth filled Jim as Julian wrapped his arms around him, holding onto him as he shot his load, Jim sandwiched between them. He turned his face toward Julian, and they kissed as Michael held them in his arms. Jim sighed as Julian pulled free of him, only to lie beside Michael, making soothing motions up and down Jim's back with his hands.

"Lie on your side, baby, facing Julian," Michael instructed.

Jim did as he was told, and Julian grabbed his leg, drawing his knee higher. Michael slid back inside him, and both held him as Michael moved in and out of him with a gentleness that was exquisite, keeping up a torrent of words: he praised Jim, told him how beautiful he was, how good it felt to be inside him…

Words that were unmistakably of love.

And when Michael came, Jim let go and tumbled with him, shooting harder than he'd believed possible, while Michael trembled against him, and Julian kissed him.

The last day of the year brought with it the most momentous moment of his life, and now Jim lay in their arms, striving to hold onto as much of Heaven as he could.

But I was right, wasn't I? That's the thing about Heaven—you don't get to keep it.

Julian met Michael's gaze across a sleeping Jim. *We wore him out*, he mouthed. Breakfast was going to become brunch, not that Julian minded. A morning ride on Jim's dick had become something quite different, and it had shaken him to the core.

Michael smiled and nodded. Then he glanced at Jim and sighed.

He feels it too.

Julian swallowed and reached over Jim to touch Michael lightly on the cheek. When he had Michael's attention, Julian looked him in the eye. *We need to talk*, he mouthed.

Michael frowned. *What's wrong?*

Another hard swallow. *I don't want him to leave.*

Chapter 15

Michael peered into the kitchen. Jim had left to spend some time writing in the cabin, promising to be back in time to see in the New Year. It had been a while since Michael and Julian had shared their New Year's celebrations with someone. Not that they did much to celebrate, other than a slow fuck by the fire with the TV on. Michael would kiss him at midnight when the ball dropped, and Julian would go off like a rocket.

Julian had gone so quiet, Michael wasn't certain he was still in the house. But there he was, making a fresh pot of coffee.

"I thought you'd be in the studio," Michael commented as he entered the kitchen.

"Maybe later." Julian didn't make eye contact, and the first tendrils of unease wound themselves around Michael's heart.

Something's wrong.

"Alone at last," he joked, hoping to lift the tension. No response.

Michael walked over to where Julian stood. "Talk to me, please." He kept his voice low, fighting to ignore the tightness in his chest and the quickening of his heartbeat.

"I can't." Still Julian wouldn't look at him, and Michael's fear bloomed.

"But you said—"

"I know what I said," Julian interjected. "But... I've

changed my mind."

Michael had had enough.

He took Julian by the shoulders and turned him slowly but firmly to face him. "Talk to me. Since when have you been unable to share with me?"

Julian swallowed. "Maybe I'm afraid of what you'll say if I do."

Oh fuck.

Michael pulled out a chair at the table and waited till Julian sat before joining him. "Now you're scaring *me.*"

"I should go do some work." Julian tried to stand, but Michael placed his hands on Julian's shoulders.

"You're staying right there until you tell me what's going on in your head."

Julian blinked. "Tell me you didn't feel it."

He frowned. "Feel what?"

"This morning. With Jim. Tell me you didn't feel that… connection. And if you do, I'll call you a fucking liar to your face."

The vehemence of his words shocked Michael into silence.

Julian dragged air into his lungs. "I'm sorry." Christ, he was shaking.

Michael took Julian's hands in his, holding them gently. "Okay. Yes, I felt it." He couldn't deny it.

"When he asked you to make love to him…" Julian shivered.

That was the moment Michael had felt it too. And sliding into him after that had been… wonderful.

"What *is* it about him that's so different?" Julian demanded. "*How* many men have been in our bed? I don't keep count, but it's a fair number. And not *one* of them has ever gotten under my skin the way he has."

"It's way past him getting under your skin." Michael cupped Julian's bearded jaw and held him steady while he gazed into the eyes he loved with every fiber of his being. "He's crawled into your heart." When Julian froze, his gaze widening, Michael nodded. "Yeah. He's in mine too."

"But..." Another hard swallow. "It's been three weeks. Three fucking weeks! How can he have...?" Julian shuddered. "Is it... because of Kristofer? Is that it? Because God, they are *so* alike."

"Yes, they are—and yet they're not. I don't know what it is about him either. I only know the more time we spend with him, the more I want to be with him." Jim's quiet ways, his laughter, his humor, his smile... All things he'd had in common with previous visitors, yet with Jim, he was *more* than the sum of those parts.

Michael gave Julian a quizzical glance. "But why should you be afraid to say all this to me? Surely you knew the effect he was having on me too. You *saw* it. You were there. I couldn't hide that." He sighed. "I couldn't deny it either."

"That wasn't why I was afraid," Julian confessed.

"Then what scares you?"

Julian's breathing hitched. "But... I said it, this morning, when he lay sleeping between us."

Michael thought back to that moment. Julian gazing at him over Jim's still form... Then it hit him.

I don't want him to leave.

"You weren't talking about him going back to the cabin, were you?"

Julian shook his head.

"You want him... to stay?"

A slow nod.

Oh Christ.

Julian paled. "You don't want that." His lip trembled, and in his neck Michael saw a visible pulse.

"I didn't say that," he fired back quickly. His mind went into overdrive. "But... he has a life. In San Francisco."

Julian's eyes flashed. "Is it making him happy? Because I don't think so. And as for his writing, he can do that anywhere. Hell, this stay in Yosemite has proved that."

Michael struggled to breathe evenly. "Look, I don't want him to go either, but..." *One* of them had to be the voice of reason. "What would you say to him? 'Hey, Jim, why don't you leave your life in San Francisco behind, move here, and live with us?' Because that's what you're suggesting, in a nutshell. And based on what? Your *gut?*"

"I know it sounds crazy. Fuck, I've told *myself* it's crazy a thousand times since I looked at him this morning, lying there. And God, it *is* crazy. Three weeks ago he walked into our life. Three lousy weeks, and yet here I am, falling in love with him." He shivered. "And the two things that scare me most? That you don't feel the same way—and neither does he." Julian drew in a deep breath, his hand trembling in Michael's. "Jesus, I just bared my fucking *soul* to you. Say *something.*"

Michael was too far away. He drew Julian into his arms and held him close, until he could feel the beat of Julian's heart. He pressed his cheek to Julian's, his arms tight around him. "Baby, I love him too. Not like I love you, because God knows I love you heart, body and soul, but yeah, I'm falling for him, so hard that it scares me." He kissed Julian's temple. "You're the one whose heart always rules their head, we both know this, but..." He took a breath as a wave of heat washed over him, leaving him light-headed in its wake. "I don't know what to do," he said simply.

Julian pulled away. "Why don't we ask Jim how he feels? Why not just ask him to stay?"

Michael's stomach clenched. "And if he says he doesn't feel the same way? What then?" He knew the answer to that. Julian's heart would break—again—only this time, Michael wouldn't be able to support him, to hold him up.

It's impossible to lift someone out of a deep hole when you're already in there with them.

Julian expelled a long breath. "Then it wasn't meant to be."

Michael blinked. "You say that *now*, but we both know it wouldn't be that easy to accept." Another calming breath. "You'd be asking him to walk away from the life he knows, to bet *everything* on a new life with us... when he's known us for so short a time. To move here, to make a new start with us..." Michael stilled. "And what about us?"

Julian's brow furrowed. "What do you mean?"

"Think about how we live, the men who drift into our life here... If two become three, what then? Will you carry on as before? Do you expect Jim to join in? What if that's not in his makeup? What if he expects monogamy?"

The silence was disturbed only by the sound of their breathing, shallow and erratic.

Julian took both Michael's hands in his. "Hear me out? Because I've been thinking this for a while. What if...?" He shuddered out a breath, then looked Michael in the eye. "I asked you a while back if you regretted coming here. You said no. Then I asked if you felt like we'd run away from the situation with Kristofer. Your response was that we came here to lick our wounds and forget him. But what if how we've chosen to live is our response to losing him?"

"What do you mean?"

"What if… we play with all these guys because we can't have *him*? I know you said you'd be happy if it was just us for the rest of our lives, but… what if there's a hole in those lives, the one he made there when he left, and all we've been doing is filling that hole, without actually acknowledging its existence?" Julian's eyes were huge. "What if Jim… completes us somehow? Not that I'm saying we're broken, okay?" He raised his eyes heavenward. "Christ, I'm really fucking this up."

Michael squeezed his hands. "No, you're not. We've been happy together for all these years. I am *never* going to fall out of love with you, you hear me? Yes, I loved Kristofer. And yes, I think I love Jim too. But the important thing is, so do you. That tells me you're not fucking this up. We're on the same page—even if I *am* the one struggling to be reasonable and logical, in a situation that makes no sense."

"So what does that mean?"

Michael let go of his hand and stroked Julian's cheek, his fingertips moving from soft skin to wiry beard. "It means we tell him how we feel… and take it from there. This is one conversation we can't plan."

"Tonight?"

Michael gaped. "It's New Year's."

"So? What better time to have this kind of conversation?" Julian's eyes shone. "I don't want to wait. Do you?"

Michael sighed. "No, I don't." He got out his phone and then stilled. "What on earth do I say to him? He already said he'd be here for midnight."

"Invite him to dinner. He won't say no to that."

Michael nodded, and his thumbs flew over the screen. Seconds later Jim's reply pinged back. "He says what time?"

"Tell him to come here for cocktails at six. We'll eat first... and then we'll see how we feel." Julian bit his lip. "You do know I'm going to be on tenterhooks until then?"

Michael kissed him. "I know. My stomach will be turning somersaults just like yours." He sent Jim the message, then set his phone down on the table.

Michael's stomach roiled. There were only two options: Jim said yes, and everything changed, or Jim said no—and everything still changed, because they'd lose him.

I don't want to lose him.

Michael had never been so scared in his life.

Chapter 16

Jim buttoned his shirt, staring at his reflection in the mirror. *When was the last time I celebrated New Year's?* Usually, he went to bed way before midnight. Celebrations were for those who had someone to celebrate *with*, and Jim had no one.

Well, you do this year.

The thought made him smile.

His phone pinged, and he grabbed it, expecting another message from Michael. When he saw Valerie's name, he stilled.

Are you busy? Can we talk?

He clicked Call. "Never too busy to talk to you."

"I just wondered what you were doing tonight. I had visions of you letting in the New Year in the middle of a forest, surrounded by bears."

He almost choked, till he remembered she was probably referring to the furrier variety of bear. Then he grinned. *Oh, I don't know. They're both pretty furry.*

"Jim? Have I lost you?"

"Yes, sorry. I zoned out for a second. I won't be on my own this evening. The owners of the cabin have invited me to celebrate with them."

"Oh, good." A pause. "So... how is the retreat going? One more week and it's back to civilization."

Jim's chest tightened. It wasn't so much the *back to civilization* part that he dreaded, but rather who he'd be leaving behind. "It's gone really well so far." Nothing like he'd anticipated. He'd expected to find solitude and inspiration, and he had, but the last thing he'd dreamed of finding was—

How the hell do I label it? Affection? Attraction? Desire?

Except it was more than that, and he knew it.

"And? Don't keep me in suspense. Have you been writing?"

Jim hadn't intended telling her until he was back home, but since she'd asked…

"I don't know what I want to do with it yet, but—"

"Publish it, I hope." She chuckled.

"Yes, but… I'm not sure who with. It's nothing like my usual stuff."

Another pause. "Jim, you've got me on the edge of my seat here. For God's sake, tell me."

He took a breath. "It's more in the line of a… romance."

An audible hitching of breath. "Seriously?"

"Oh, it's gets worse. A gay romance."

Crickets.

Oh God. She hates the idea.

"Okay, it's not like Harlequin or something of that ilk," he added quickly. "It's just the story of two men. How they meet, what draws them together, what threatens to split them apart… And I *have* been thinking seriously about self-publishing it, because I couldn't see my publisher going for it."

"You're acquainted with the hash-tag Own Voices? Dumb question, of course you are. You write about a pair of gay detectives. Have you *any idea* how big the romance market is? So any romance publisher would *jump* at the chance to have an Own Voices author."

Her words sank in. "Wait a minute. You know I'm

gay? Not *once* have I said I'm gay."

Silence.

"Valerie?" Fuck, did his *publisher* know?

She sighed. "Okay, I sort of… had a feeling. Come on, I've known you for a *decade*, Jim. I'm like your surrogate mom. I didn't ask, because you obviously didn't want to tell, but this… And before you ask, I haven't shared my suspicions with a *soul*."

He breathed a little easier.

"So would you publish it under the same pen name? Or your own?"

Jim laughed. "Whoa. It isn't even finished yet."

"And I'm excited already. I want to read what you've written so far."

"You *know* I hate doing that. I'll send it to you when it's done, and not before."

Valerie made a gleeful sound. "Oh, I like the sound of this. Come see me when you get back to San Francisco, and we'll talk some more."

Jim chuckled. "Happy New Year for when it reaches you."

"You too. Write more words!"

He disconnected. *Well, I think I made Valerie's day.* The evening lay before him, and he couldn't wait. He wasn't anticipating anything more than a night spent in good company, with maybe a kiss or two at midnight.

Yeah right. Do I really think they're going to send me back to my cabin once midnight has come and gone? It would be the first time in almost two weeks if they did.

He wondered what Michael and Julian would make of his new book. Both his characters were bruised by their pasts, and Michael and Julian had their share of bruises. *Does that make them more attractive?* It certainly gave him the desire to wrap them both in his arms and hold them.

His phone *pinged* again, and this time it was Michael.

Come when you're ready.

Jim smiled. *Seems as if I'm not the only one who's looking forward to tonight.* He intended to make the most of his last week, to burn every precious second into his memory.

I want to hold onto them for as long as I can.

Jim pushed away his plate with a sigh. "That was delicious."

"Hey, it was only pot roast," Julian said with a modest wave.

"Yes, but I'm a sucker for a good pot roast. We're talking the way to *this* man's heart." His light-hearted comment didn't hit its mark: there was still tension in the air. It had been obvious the minute Jim stepped across their threshold. Nothing overt, just a sense that something was simmering below the surface. Michael's smiles continually wavered. Julian was quieter, less animated. When there was no dissipation throughout dinner, he came to the conclusion he'd walked in on an argument that had yet to culminate. Why else were they avoiding direct eye contact with each other?

They don't need me around them. They need space.

Jim put down his napkin with a sigh. "Listen, I should go."

Two pairs of eyes regarded him in obvious alarm.

"Don't," Julian blurted. "Please. We want you to stay."

"We were going to watch a movie," Michael added. "Please, stay?"

For a moment it occurred to Jim that they wanted him for a buffer, and he balked at the idea. But they so plainly wanted him there, he didn't have the heart to refuse.

"What's the movie?"

"Don't laugh. It's really old, but it's sort of a tradition," Julian told him. "The first New Year's we spent together, we stayed up till three in the morning, putting the world to rights—and watching a movie called *Duck Soup*."

Jim blinked. "The Marx Brothers?" Okay, he hadn't expected that.

Julian stared at him. "You are *way* too young to even know who the Marx Brothers were."

He grinned. "My grandmother loved them. She had these cute little figurines of them in her cabinet." He gave a dramatic sigh. "You have *no* idea how disillusioned I was when I discovered Groucho's mustache wasn't real."

They both laughed, and Jim heaved an internal sigh of relief.

Michael nodded. "Every New Year's since then, we watch one of their movies."

Jim looked from Michael to Julian, noting how they both fidgeted, how Julian jittered his foot against the floor, and how Michael glanced anxiously at the wall clock.

Something is definitely *going on.* And he wanted to know.

"So what's this year's movie?"

"*Animal Crackers*." Michael gave a pointed stare in Julian's direction. "His choice."

Jim forced a chuckle. "I always liked *Night at the Opera* myself."

Michael widened his eyes. "And that's *my* favorite."

"It sure is." Julian rolled his eyes. "It was always the same. We'd go out to eat, I'd order, and after every item, *this* one would add, 'And two hard-boiled eggs.' Confused the servers all to hell."

"Then it's settled. I'll get the popcorn, Julian will pour us a drink, and we'll watch the movie." Michael's eyes twinkled. "Let's see how many movies we can watch before midnight."

"Sounds like a plan." Jim had a feeling he'd have a small, furry lap cushion, and that was fine by him. Buster didn't fuss, but made himself comfortable and went to sleep. At his age, he was allowed to.

Ten minutes later, the three of them were on the couch, Jim in the middle, with a bowl of popcorn on each side of him. Buster sniffed at the bowls, then lowered his head. As the opening credits rolled, Jim took a moment to assess the situation.

Did I get it wrong?

Then he listened to the sound of their breathing. It was shallow and erratic.

No. He hadn't imagined it.

By the time midnight was only ten minutes away, they'd watched three movies. Well, *Jim* had watched them—he got the sense that Michael and Julian were half-watching. Julian got up from the couch to open the bottle of champagne that was apparently another tradition. He popped the cork and filled three flutes.

"We *have* varied our New Year's traditions in one

respect," Michael told Jim as he handed him a glass.

"Oh?"

Michael bit his lip. "We're usually naked by this point. We like to start the New Year with a bang— literally."

Jim gave him a mock glare. "Hey, I'm missing out here."

They laughed. Then Julian pointed to the TV. "Quick, turn the sound up. It's almost midnight."

Jim chuckled. "You know it's recorded, right? All those people in Times Square are probably in bed by now."

"Hey, don't shatter my illusions." The three of them stood with their glasses raised as the crowd counted down, and on the stroke of midnight, Michael and Julian kissed. Jim felt a bit awkward, until they pulled him into a three-way kiss that sent his heartbeat racing.

Maybe he wasn't about to miss out on one tradition after all.

When they released him, they clinked glasses, and Jim drank a little of the deliciously chilled champagne. He sighed. "Well, this is the first New Year's in a long time where I'm not alone. Maybe it's a precursor of change."

Michael glanced at Julian, and the hairs stood up on Jim's arms.

What just happened?

"Jim, sit down please." Julian gestured to the couch.

The quietness of his voice was unnerving.

Jim sat, his heart pounding. "Something's wrong. I've felt it all night." Michael and Julian flanked him on the couch, and the hush that fell only served to ramp up his anxiety. "Please. This is killing me. Whatever it is you're trying so hard not to say, for God's sake, *tell* me."

Michael took his hand. "We've loved having you around these last few weeks."

He forced himself to breathe. "And I've loved being here. You have *no* idea. You two have… well, you've changed everything." Understatement of the year—except the year was mere minutes old.

"You've changed us too," Julian said softly.

He frowned. "In what way?" Surely he was the latest in a long line of guys who meandered through their lives, warming their bed. And yet he knew that wasn't true. Michael had all but confessed that none of the others had received an open invitation to their home. Jim also knew being invited to their studios to watch them work was something else they hadn't done with all those other guys.

So why me? What makes me so special?

Maybe he was about to find out.

Julian looked him in the eye. "When we're in bed, the three of us… there's been a connection."

Jim caught his breath.

"But it's not just in bed," Michael continued, his face as grave as Julian's, his gaze as unwavering.

Oh fuck.

"And what we want to ask you… is if you've felt it too." Julian swallowed. "Because if you *have*…"

Jim's heart hammered.

Julian let out a low growl. "Fuck this tiptoeing around. Jim… we're falling in love with you. We hope to God you're falling for us. And we want you to come live here, with us. Move in. Share our lives."

Holy fucking God.

Michael rolled his eyes. "Yeah, that was about as subtle as a train wreck." He tightened his grip on Jim's hand. "Okay, every word he said was true. You're a very special man, Jim Traynor, and we don't want to lose you. I know this makes no sense, not when we've known you for less than a month, but—"

"We had to say *something*." Julian cupped Jim's chin and turned him to meet Julian's earnest gaze. "Like Michael says, we don't want to lose you. We *need* you, more than you can know."

Oh God. He suddenly understood where this was coming from.

"I am *not* a replacement for Kristofer, all right?" As soon as the words left his lips, Jim knew he'd gotten it wrong. Their dual expressions of horror...

"Fuck no." Michael gave him a pained stare. "We don't think that, I promise. And we wouldn't *want* you to be."

"Are we reading this all wrong?" Julian demanded. "Look at me, and tell me you feel nothing for us."

He couldn't do that. He'd be the biggest fucking liar on the planet.

Jim fought to remain calm. "Jesus, guys, give me a chance to breathe. You just hit the gas and we went from zero to one hundred miles per hour in about two-point-three seconds flat." *Move here? Live with them? Are they serious?* One glance at their faces told him the truth.

They really want this.

"What's waiting for you back in San Francisco?" Julian's voice had lost its rough edge. "You don't have family there, do you? It's just you. And you can write anywhere."

"I'm sure we can come up with a dozen reasons why you should stay." Michael drew in a deep breath.

"But if it's not what you want…"

Jim took in Julian's urgency, Michael's watchful expression… His chest was so fucking tight, and his heart felt like it was about to explode.

What was killing him most was the speed of it all.

Jim shuddered out a breath. "Guys… I need to go back to the cabin." He had to get out there. He needed space to breathe, to think.

"Now?" Jesus, the hurt in Julian's eyes…

"No, Jim's right." Michael, the voice of calm. He laid a hand on Jim's arm. "We did just drop a bombshell, after all. Go back to the cabin. Think about it."

Jim got to his feet. "Thank you." God, he was trembling.

"Just so long as you know…" Julian lifted his chin and locked gazes with him. "We won't have changed our minds by morning."

"Julian…" Michael said softly.

Jim hurried to the front door and grabbed his coat from the hook. He threw his scarf around his neck, stuffed his feet into his boots, and then turned to face them. "I just need time, okay?"

Michael nodded. "We understand."

Jim was glad *someone* did, because this whole business had his head reeling.

He walked out into the cold night air, deliberately not looking back at the house as he passed in front of the windows. He couldn't think around Michael and Julian. They addled his brain. They messed up his logic circuits.

We need you, more than you can know.

The pressure in one simple statement…

I can't be that critical to their happiness. I just can't.

What if I can't be what they need?
Christ, I've never been in a relationship.

That last thought stopped him dead in the middle of the snow-covered lane, and he shivered. *You fool. You're in one now. What do you call what's been happening the last few weeks, if not a relationship?*

Except there was a heap of difference between that, and what Michael and Julian were proposing.

There's a reason I've never gotten involved with anyone. Why I never wanted all these emotional entanglements. They drain people. They sap energy. They take up time.

He swallowed. *And they hurt when they go wrong.*

Not that he'd ever experienced that pain. He'd done his best to keep that particular wolf from his door. He'd avoided people, relationships—love…

And yet love had snuck up on him, delivering a wallop that knocked the air from his lungs, made his head spin and his heart ache.

Christ, I can't think straight.

Jim resumed his hurried pace, putting distance between him and the two men who'd just done the bravest thing he'd ever known. They'd taken an enormous gamble.

Am I prepared to take as big a leap into the unknown?

Jim didn't know.

By the time five a.m. rolled around, Julian had slept maybe an hour. Michael had tossed and turned beside him, and when he sat up in bed, put on a robe, and declared he was getting up, Julian gave up all hope of sleep.

"Me too. I'll make coffee."

He wandered into the kitchen. The dishes from the previous night still sat there: he hadn't had sufficient motivation to load them into the dishwasher. Michael removed the bag of bagels from the cabinet and removed a couple.

Julian wasn't sure he could eat. His throat felt tight.

"Do you think he's sleeping?"

"I doubt it. He's probably as wound up as we are." Michael sighed. "And now I'm asking myself if we did the wrong thing, blurting it out the way we did."

Julian had had the same thought. "It's all my fault. I shouldn't have gone in all guns blazing." He spooned coffee into the filter. "God, his face… Maybe we should've left things as they were, let him finish his stay, before we dropped it all on him." Now they had the prospect of one week before his departure. *Have we made things really awkward?*

Julian needed to know.

He grabbed the notepad from its hook next to the fridge, and removed the pen from its holder.

"What are you doing?" Michael asked as he spread cream cheese over the sliced bagels.

"Writing Jim a note, which *you* are going to put under his door," he said decisively.

Michael paused. "Saying what? Give him some space, baby. He said he needed time."

"And I'm giving him that. I'm also giving him the option of joining us for lunch today." Julian kept the note short and sweet. He folded it and held it out to Michael, who gazed at him with arched eyebrows.

"What—it can't wait until after we've eaten? Or had coffee?"

"No, it can't." Julian stared back. "Please, Michael. I have to do something."

Michael's shoulders sagged. "I know. I feel the same way." He glanced at his robe. "Let me put on some clothes first? I'll take Buster with me."

Julian kissed him. "Thank you." He went back to making the coffee.

Five minutes later, he caught the sound of the front door closing, and he breathed a little easier. The note hadn't said much, only invited him to lunch, but at the end Julian had written:

I'm sorry. I know we rushed you into this, but please, don't hold it against us.

Julian

His stomach roiled. *Have we messed things up beyond hope of repair?*

God, he hoped not.

Ten minutes later, his phone rang. When he saw Michael's name, a ribbon of unease wound itself around his heart and tightened. "What's wrong?" he demanded as soon as the call connected.

"Jim's not here."

"What do you mean? Has he gone for a walk?"

"I mean, he's gone. The cabin is empty and his car isn't in its space. He must have gone sometime in the night." A pause. "Wait a sec. He left us a note."

His heart quaked. "What does it say?"

Michael's voice shook. "Michael and Julian, please don't hate me for leaving without letting you know. I think I understand what it took for you to admit your feelings, I just need time to figure me/this/us out. Jim."

"He said 'us'?" Julian clung to the one word that provided a glimmer of hope. Because God knew he needed that right then.

"Oh God, this is a mess."

Julian breathed deeply. "Come home. All we can do is wait."

Chapter 17

Jim sipped his Gingersnap iced coffee, relishing its sweetness and creamy texture. It was too damn cold outside for iced coffee, but inside Philz the temperature was perfect. He sat at the huge wooden table, his phone and laptop plugged into it, and gazed through the window at the hustle and bustle of downtown San Francisco.

I didn't miss this.

Two weeks since he'd returned from Yosemite, and Jim had seen—and heard—enough traffic to last a lifetime.

Then why did I come down here? For God's sake, it's rush hour out there.

Except he knew why, and it had nothing to do with meeting Valerie.

And speak of the devil...

Valerie smiled at him through the glass, then hurried inside. Jim got up to give her a hug. "What do you want to drink? I can recommend the Tesoro. It's a great flavor."

She chuckled. "If it's coffee, I'm pretty much sold, but sit down. I'll get it." She glanced at the display of pastries. "There's also a muffin that has my name on it. Do *you* want one?"

He was about to refuse, then changed his mind. "Yeah, why not?"

Valerie blinked. "I asked, because I always do, but

then again, you always refuse. Who are you, and what have you done with Jim Traynor?" Her eyes sparkled.

He gave her a playful shove toward the counter. "Get your coffee." Then he retook his seat. The table wasn't as full as usual—there were times when eight to ten people squeezed in around it, staring at phones or laptops. Jim had been coming there every day for the past two weeks, with only one purpose.

I want to remember this.

He told himself he hadn't come to a decision. His life felt as if it were on hold. He hadn't written a word. When Valerie had called a couple of days after New Year's to check on his progress, he'd told her flat out he wasn't sure he could finish the book, or if it was even *worth* completing. Then he'd disconnected the call.

As if that would deter her. She'd emailed him, demanding to read what he'd written thus far, and telling him she'd be the judge of its worth, or the lack thereof. When she'd sent three emails, Jim threw in the towel and sent the manuscript to her.

It had been radio silence since then, and that scared the shit out of him.

Her call that morning to ask him to meet for a coffee had set his heart hammering, but he'd agreed. And now she was here, someone was playing a drum military tattoo in his chest.

Valerie sat in the empty chair facing him, and placed the two muffins between them on napkins. "I got a blueberry one, and a raspberry and white chocolate." She narrowed her eyes. "Choose the latter, and you're a dead man."

Jim laughed and pulled the blueberry muffin toward him.

Valerie glanced at their surroundings. "Tell me

again why we're here."

"What—this location?" She nodded. "Call it therapy. Negative reinforcement. Whatever."

She frowned. "I don't understand."

Jim wasn't sure he did either.

Valerie ignored her muffin, placed her elbows on the table, and rested her chin on laced fingers. "We need to talk about this book."

He swallowed, then arched his eyebrows. "Isn't that why we're meeting?"

"I've been doing some research. I know you said you'd thought about self-publishing it, but there's an option I think you should consider. I found a new publishing company that's worth a look. They're asking for submissions with diverse characters, and they have an LGBTQA+ line." She smiled. "Your book would be perfect for them. You would be a good fit."

He caught his breath. "Then you think I should finish it."

She gave a slow nod. "I have to say… Mike and Jake…" She pushed out a long sigh.

"What about them?"

"Don't get me wrong. I *loved* Gary and Mick, but with them, it was always the business of murder, finding the clues, solving the case. Mike and Jake felt more… alive to me, more real, in one incomplete manuscript, than Gary and Mick did after countless books." She looked into his eyes. "And I want to know why."

"What do you mean?" That one sentence had set off a horde of rampaging butterflies in his stomach.

"They're amazing characters. They're fully fleshed-out. Hell, I want to meet them, to *hug* them. And they're nothing like any characters you've ever written. So I have to ask…" She hadn't broken eye contact. "Are they based on anyone in particular?"

Jim stared at her, his stomach roiling.

The young woman behind the counter called out "Tesoro, sweet."

"That's me." Valerie got up and went over to collect her coffee.

He took several deep breaths, attempting to calm himself. By the time she'd retaken her seat, he'd made up his mind.

"I need to tell you about Yosemite," he said in a low voice.

Valerie stilled. "Only if you want to." When he gave her an inquiring glance, she shrugged. "I know *something* happened there. The manuscript was proof of that."

He started at the beginning, with Buster's welcome intrusion, and told her everything, right up to the note he'd left for them. Valerie listened in silence, drinking her coffee and pulling pieces off her muffin, her gaze rarely leaving him. When he was done, he sagged into his chair, mentally exhausted.

Valerie exhaled. "Wow."

He bit his lip. "That's all it warrants? Wow? My world just got turned upside-down."

"Has either of them been in touch since you left?"

Jim smiled. "I've had a total of two emails, both saying the same thing."

"Come back?" she said with a smile.

He shook his head. "'Are you all right?'"

"Did you reply?"

"I told them I was fine."

"And they left it at that? Then they really *are* giving you space to make up your own mind." Valerie cocked her head to one side. "And have you?"

His throat seized and he couldn't answer.

Valerie rested her chin on her hands again. "Want to hear *my* thoughts on the subject?"

"I figured you'd share them anyway, whether I wanted to listen or not."

She beamed. "You know me *so* well." She drank a little more coffee. "Okay. From a purely practical angle, Julian nailed it. You can work anywhere. All you need is the Internet, and *that*." She pointed to his laptop. "Have you written anything since you came home?"

He shook his head.

"And that segues nicely into my next point. San Francisco isn't home—it's the place where you happen to live. I don't think you have any emotional attachments to it." The tilt of the head again. "Am I wrong?"

"No, you're not wrong."

"Did you like Yosemite?"

He sighed. "Like, no. Love? Yes."

She nodded. "Which brings me to your men."

He blinked. "*My* men?"

"Yes, yours. That book is full of them, and don't deny it. So two gorgeous men—they *are* gorgeous, aren't they?"

He chuckled. "If you're into bears, then yes, they're…." He swallowed. "Beautiful."

Valerie reached across the table and took his hand, squeezing it. She didn't relinquish it, however. "So… two gorgeous men tell you they're falling in love with you, and ask you to come live with them in a place you love, that obviously inspires you…" Her eyes twinkled. "Tell me what I'm not seeing here. Because from where *I'm* sitting, it sounds idyllic."

"I suppose it does, but there's more to it than

that."

She gripped his hand. "Then *tell* me. What's preventing you from packing everything you own into your car, and driving—how many hours?"

"Four, give or take."

She nodded. "Okay, driving four hours to land on their doorstep, throw your arms around them, and say, 'I'm yours'?" She narrowed her gaze. "And *don't* tell me you're afraid you'll just be a replacement for this Kristofer guy. Michael refuted that. They both did."

"I'm just afraid." Terrified was nearer the mark.

"Of what?" Valerie's grip on his hand softened, as did her voice. "Tell me what you're so scared of."

"My actions could hurt them."

She blinked. "How?"

"They say they need me. That's a lot of pressure. What if... what if I can't be to them what they need? What if it doesn't work out, and I have to leave?"

Valerie sighed. "Let's leave the 'What-ifs' out of this for the moment." She took a drink. "You need to go into this with your eyes open, *knowing* it might not last forever." She locked gazes with him. "But it could. Yes, people change, and nothing is permanent, but... isn't it worth the risk? Don't you think you'd regret *not* trying?" She smiled. "What do they say? 'Better to have loved and lost...'"

"And that's just it. I've never loved anyone. I've never lost anyone."

"Then maybe you've never really lived—you've just *existed*."

That stopped him in his tracks.

"And another thing. They've been together a very long time, and yet they feel strongly enough about you to invite you into their lives. They must know there are no guarantees, but they're willing to take a chance."

"Yes, but…" Jim drew in a deep breath. "Will they expect to continue their life as it is now? Inviting men to their bed when they feel a spark of desire?"

"You're asking *me*? How the hell should *I* know? *They're* the only ones who can answer that, and yes, you'd need to talk about that." Valerie's eyes shone. "What if they're bringing guys to their bed to fill a hole in their lives they don't even know exists—a hole that *you* fit into perfectly?"

He'd had the same thought, usually in the middle of the night when he couldn't sleep. There hadn't been a lot of sleep in the last fourteen days, and he was almost running on empty.

"One final observation, and then I'll leave you to your thoughts."

Jim had done too much thinking lately.

Valerie let go of his hand and leaned back in her chair. "I think you've already made up your mind—you just haven't realized it yet."

He widened his eyes. "Enlighten me."

"You told me you've been coming down here a lot." When he nodded, she gestured to the world beyond the coffee shop window. "But you *hate* this. The noise, the traffic, the overpopulation… And yet you come here, again and again. It may be a subconscious decision. Except *I* think I know why."

Breathing became difficult, his attention focused on her, awaiting the confirmation of his own assumptions.

"I think you're making deposits in a sort of Bad Memory Bank. You're subjecting yourself to negative experiences, not because you're a masochist, but because at some later date, you're going to make a withdrawal from that bank. You're going to remind yourself of all the things you left behind—when you moved to Yosemite."

His breathing hitched. "Fuck," he said softly.

She stared at him. "All this time we've been talking, there's one thing you haven't told me."

His heart raced.

Valerie raised her chin and met his gaze. "Are *you* in love with *them*?"

"How would I know? I've never loved anyone, remember?" Except he was hedging, and he knew it.

Valerie didn't look away. "Do they make your pulse race, your heart hammer? Do they make you feel weak at the knees? Does something flutter in your stomach when you're away from them, a feeling of emptiness? Do you find yourself smiling when you think about them? And *don't* tell me you don't know what love is, because it *permeates* that book you haven't finished yet. How else do you think you were able to write it? Because you're writing about *yourself*, you idiot."

His throat tightened.

Valerie gave him a knowing smile. "I love being right. So listen to me, Jim Traynor. Go back to your tiny, rent-controlled apartment, find every box you can lay your hands on—and I have an attic-full, if you need more—and pack up whatever possessions mean something to you. The rest, put it in a dumpster or give it to Goodwill. Then make a Thermos full of coffee, buy a load of snacks, and hit the road, Jack." She grinned. "And don't you come back no more."

He laughed, overwhelmed by a sudden onslaught of giddiness. "It's that simple, is it?"

"It is if you make it so." She grinned and got to her

feet. "I'm going now. Call me when you finish the book—and send me a postcard from Yosemite." She walked around the table, bent down, and kissed his cheek. "Be happy," she whispered. And with that, she straightened, pulled her coat tight around her, and strode out into the chilly January wind.

Jim stared at his laptop, his heart pounding.

Can it be that simple?

There was only one way to find out.

Michael locked the door, then went into the living room. "Where's Buster?" he called out.

"Already on the bed."

No surprise there. Buster had slept with them every night since... He sighed. *He misses Jim too.* Except missing him didn't even come close. There had been a hollowness in Michael's chest for two weeks. He ached, yet had nothing to point to as the cause. Fatigue followed him throughout the day, and as for working... At least he'd finished his carving of Jim. He just couldn't look at it.

Julian, on the other hand, seemed to be painting up a storm in his studio, not that he'd let Michael inside. *Maybe that's his coping mechanism.* And when night fell and they pulled the comforter over them, they held each other, neither of them uttering his name. Yet for Michael, Jim was still there. He could see him lying on their bed, kissing Julian, while Michael slid in and out of his body at a gentle, sensual pace, making love to their boy.

"Michael."

He blinked. He'd been zoning out a lot recently. "Yes?"

"A car just pulled onto the driveway." Michael heard the thud of Julian's feet on the stairs, and Julian burst into the room, tying the belt around his dark blue robe. One glance at Julian's face told him whose car it was, and he ran to the door, his fingers trembling as he fumbled with the lock. He flung it open and stepped out into the bright glare of the security light that flooded the graveled drive. Julian was close behind him, and from upstairs Michael heard Buster's bark.

He's back. Warmth radiated throughout Michael's body, and all fatigue fled. *But for how long?* Then he took a good look at Jim's car, and laughter burst out of him. It was packed to the roof.

Jim got out, and closed the car door. "Hey." He gave them an adorably shy smile. "I didn't reserve a cabin this time. I don't think it would take all this anyway."

That was as far as Michael let him go before he closed the distance between them, and took Jim in his arms. Then Julian joined him, and three mouths met in a fierce kiss.

Jim shivered against them, and Michael kissed his forehead.

"Welcome home."

Chapter 18

Julian still couldn't believe it. Jim was *really* there, sitting between them on the couch, Buster on his lap, clamoring for more head rubs. "You have *no* idea how much I hoped for this. The effort it took not to call you…"

Jim chuckled. "Frankly, your restraint amazed me."

"But I didn't want you to take restraint for—"

Jim silenced his words with a finger. "Hey, it's okay. I didn't take the lack of communication as a sign you didn't care. Quite the opposite. You did what you promised. You gave me time."

"These two weeks have been the longest of my life," Michael murmured. "The only thing that kept me sane was…" He grabbed his phone from the coffee table, scrolled, and then thrust it into Jim's hands.

Jim's sharp intake of breath mirrored Julian's, the first time he'd seen the result of Michael's labors. "Oh my God…"

"He captured so much of you," Julian said in a low voice, glancing at the photo of Michael's wood carving.

"It's breathtaking." Jim wiped his eyes. "So beautiful."

Michael took the phone from him. "That's because it's you." He returned it to the coffee table. "Are you sure about this?"

When Jim didn't reply instantly, Julian took hold of his hands. "Are there a few things you'd like to get clear first? Any questions, for instance? I know we're asking a lot of you."

"Sure, there are practicalities, such as… we're going to share the bills, right?"

Michael smiled. "Yes, we can do that. And about your work… I've been thinking a lot about that since you went."

"Since I walked out without telling you I was going, you mean." Jim's face tightened. "I'm sorry about that. I just panicked. That damn hamster in my brain was going so fast in that fucking wheel, I swear it was going to catch fire. I had to get out of there."

This time Julian silenced him with a kiss. "You're here now. That's all that matters. You're here… with us."

"That's one of the things I want to discuss." Jim cleared his throat. "Look, I know you said if you only had each other for the rest of your lives, it would be enough, and I know you said the guys who come along are just the icing on the cake… but what I need to know is…"

Julian saw where he was heading. "You want to know if we'll still want to invite guys to share our bed." Jim nodded.

Michael sighed. "I've been thinking about this too. We both have." He cupped Jim's chin and turned his face toward Michael. "I don't think you'd be happy with that. And now? I'm not sure I would either."

"So I'm going to say no. No more invitations." Julian's lips twitched. "But I'm *not* going to say never, simply because the day might come when a guy comes to stay, and you turn to us and say, 'Wow, he is *gorgeous*.'"

Jim laughed. "I can live with that."

"Can I tell you my idea now?" Michael's voice held a plaintive note, and both Julian and Jim laughed. "Okay. Did you know George Bernard Shaw had a writing shed that revolved so he could follow the sun?"

Jim blinked. "That was... random."

"Hear me out. He had a desk in there, it had power, a bed so he could take a nap whenever he felt so inclined... It was his own little world where he went to write. So I got to thinking... There's enough land out back for a writing room. I could build that for you. That way, we'd each have a work space."

Jim stared at him. "You'd go to all that trouble... for me?"

"Of course." Michael stroked his cheek. "Anything for the man I love."

"The man *we* love," Julian corrected him.

Jim shuddered out a breath. "I met with my agent this morning. She asked me if I was in love with you." He paused. "I think it was meeting you two that taught me how to love."

Julian caught his breath, waiting for the words, and it was as if Jim sensed the tension in him. Jim took their hands in his. "And yes, I love you too."

The moment the words left his lips, Michael claimed Jim's mouth in a fervent kiss, yielding to Julian seconds later.

When they sat back, Jim shivered. "You'll have to be patient with me. When it comes to relationships, I'm—"

"In virgin territory." Julian nodded. "We know. But remember, so are we. We've never done this either." When Jim regarded him in obvious surprise, he smiled. "Kristofer never lived with us."

"I know I called him 'the boy who stayed',"

Michael added, "but the truth is, he only stayed now and then. I also said we left the cage door open, remember? The problem with that, is that sometimes the bird wants to fly away for a while. We wanted more, not that we ever told him that."

"And he *never* turned up with a car loaded with all his possessions." Julian swallowed. "Just seeing that? I wanted to cry."

"Valerie said I had to go into this knowing it might not last forever."

"And she's right," Michael said, his voice gentle. "There are no absolutes in life. We just need to remember to share what's in our hearts. If something bothers you, or worries you, say so."

"It'll take time to adjust, I'm sure of that, for all of us," Julian murmured. "But don't forget the one thing that binds us together."

Jim nodded. "Love."

Julian's heart felt as though it was about to burst. "Sorry, but this couch won't do. I want to hold you in my arms, kiss you, touch you."

"Is there still a Jim-sized space in that big bed of yours?" Jim asked with a shy smile.

Michael got to his feet and held out his hand. "Why don't we go and find out?"

"But what about all my stuff out there in the car?"

Julian laughed. "It'll still be there in the morning—unless of course the bears and squirrels decide to investigate, because they *really* like the look of something in there. We've got a new toothbrush up there for you, none of us wear pajamas... Is there anything you badly need tonight?"

Jim shook his head, and Michael helped him up off the couch. He led Jim toward the stairs, Julian following. When Buster followed too, Julian bent down and stroked the little dog.

"I don't think this is going to be a Let's-cuddle-Buster night," he said in a low voice. Then he hurried after Michael and Jim. When he reached the bedroom, Jim was standing at the foot of the bed, staring at the wall.

"At the risk of repeating myself…Oh my God."

Julian joined him, his hand to Jim's back. "I thought the portrait of our friends Ben and Anthony was the best thing I'd ever done." He gestured to the square canvas. "This beats it." It was like nothing he'd ever attempted: the three of them lying down, seen from the waist up, but with Jim locked between them, Michael above him, the muscles in his arms straining.

Jim shivered. "It's as if… you caught us all on camera, the moment we…"

Julian nodded. "That was the idea." He gazed at his handiwork. "I don't think I came out of the studio except to sleep. I had to finish it. That was three days ago. And I haven't stopped looking at it since."

Jim's eyes shone. "Both of you…. So fucking talented." Then he lowered his gaze to the bed.

"Tell me what you're thinking."

Jim swallowed. "So… are there rules?"

He blinked. "Rules about what?"

"Well… does it have to be all three of us, every time we make love? I mean, you had that playing together rule, right? Say I wanted to go into Michael's studio and… fool around. Would that be okay?"

Julian frowned. "Why would that not be okay? Except of course, *I'd* expect the same courtesy at some point."

Michael joined them. "Where did you get that idea

from?"

"Something I read while I was… away from you."

Julian bit back a smile. "What the hell have you been reading?"

"It was a gay ménage romance. Call it… research. And they could only fuck if it was all three of them."

Michael chuckled. "No. No rules like that. The only rule around here? Be honest with each other about what we want, what we need…"

"No," Julian said suddenly. "He's got a point." When both of them turned to face him, he nodded. "Maybe I'd add a rule that says if two of us are making love… it's okay for the other to watch." He grinned.

"And we'll need to discuss testing too." Jim looked from Michael to Julian. "You get tests done regularly, right? So I need to start doing that too."

When he fell silent, Julian cupped his chin. "Is that it? No more questions?"

"For now, no. I'm sure there will be others, but right now I just want what I've been dreaming about for two weeks." Jim leaned in and kissed Julian on the lips, then did the same with Michael.

Then Michael's expression sobered. "You're still our boy?"

Jim's breathing hitched. "Still yours, Daddy."

They had to be the sweetest words ever.

Julian straddled Michael's hips while they kissed, and Jim laid a trail of kisses down Julian's spine. When he reached Julian's furry cleft, Julian reached back and spread his cheeks.

"Get me ready?"

Jim smiled. "I'll get both of you ready." He licked a path over Julian's hole, his hand around the base of Michael's dick, working the silken shaft. Then he took Michael into his mouth, loving Michael's moan of pleasure. Jim alternated between them, pushing the tip of his tongue deeper into Julian's warmth, then sucking on the wide, taut head, teasing Julian's hole. He squeezed lube along Michael's cock, guided it into position, and Julian sank down on it, while Jim licked and kissed the skin where it was stretched tight around Michael's girth. Then he shifted, kneeling beside Julian on the bed, Jim's arms around him, kissing his lips, his throat, his nape, across his shoulders, while Julian rocked back and forth, impaling himself leisurely on Michael's thick shaft.

"Love watching you kiss," Michael said softly, pushing up with his hips. Julian threw his head back and Jim pressed his lips to Julian's neck, kissing and sucking him there, pulling groans that sent the blood heading to Jim's dick.

They didn't stay in one position for any length of time, and that was just perfect. Jim wanted to fill his *soul* with all their permutations: whether it was him mounting Julian and sliding into him while Michael filled Jim to the hilt; Jim riding Michael's shaft while Julian swallowed Jim's cock to the root; Michael sheathing his dick in Julian's body while Jim lay beside Julian, the pair of them kissing, Michael's fingers wedged in Jim's ass, massaging his prostate until Jim was crying out with the pleasure of it all: or that exquisite moment when Jim lay on his back, Julian's cock gliding in and out of his mouth while Julian and Michael kissed, and Jim came without a touch to his dick.

So many kisses to catch up on.

Jim had known before they'd reached the bed that there was one experience he wanted to relive. He pushed Julian gently onto his back, then straddled his hips, reaching back to guide Julian's thick cock into his hole. Jim propped himself up on his hands and gazed into Julian's eyes.

"I want you both. Want to feel both my Daddies inside me."

Julian's breathing hitched, and he locked his arms around Jim's neck, pulling him down into a fierce kiss that robbed him of air. Michael's hand was gentle on his back, pushing him down, and then he was there, the heat of him pressing slowly into Jim's body, Julian so still beneath him, and Jim couldn't hold in his joy a second longer. He wanted to weep as Michael slid into him, feeling so stretched and so loved.

And when they came inside him, Jim locked between their bodies, both men whispering words of love to him, he couldn't hold back the tears.

For the first time in his life, he was truly home.

The End

New from KC

Maine Men

Levi, Noah, Aaron, Ben, Dylan, Finn, Seb, and Shaun.

Eight friends who grew up in Wells, Maine.

Different backgrounds, different paths, but one thing remains solid, even eight years after they graduated – their friendship. Holidays, weddings, funerals, birthdays, parties – any chance they get to meet up, they take it. It's an opportunity to share what's going on in their lives, especially their love lives.

Back in high school, they knew four of them were gay or bi, so maybe it was more than coincidence that they gravitated to one another. Along the way, there were revelations and realizations, some more of a surprise than others. And what none of the others knew was that Levi was in love with one of them...

Finn's Fantasy

A secret desire

By day, Finn builds houses on the coastline of Maine. Afterhours, Finn dreams of the hot older guy who walks his chocolate lab on Goose Rocks Beach. The man of his dreams ticks all his boxes. Salt and pepper hair. Strong jawline. Blue eyes. His dream man is perfect fantasy material. As for actually speaking to him? As if. Their paths won't ever cross, and the guy is probably straight.

A new chapter

Recently divorced Joel is finally living as a gay man, but he's not sure he's ready to jump into a relationship. That doesn't stop him from noticing his new contractor's muscular build, hewn from hard, physical work, or his storm-colored eyes. Or the way he wears his tool belt slung low on his hips. The icing on the cake? There's more to Finn than good looks. Maybe he's the perfect guy to share long walks on the beach and warm nights in front of a fire.

But it's been twenty years since Joel was with a man. While he's not forgotten how to flirt, he's nervous about making a move.

Especially with Finn.

Ben's Boss

"Pearson's a common name."
"It can't be him."
"God wouldn't be that cruel."

A painful history

Walking into the job interview confirms Ben White's worst fears. It's been eight years since high school, yet he can still recall Wade Pearson's taunts.

There's always a chance Wade isn't the same homophobic asshole Ben knew. *Yeah right.*

Except the boy Ben remembers has grown into one seriously hot, brooding man. In another life, Ben would have climbed him like a tree. Wade's gaze still makes Ben shiver – although now for entirely different reasons.

A secret longing

As soon as Wade read Ben's application, he knew he had to see him. Ben's still as gorgeous as Wade remembers. It's obvious he doesn't expect to get the job, given their history.

But Wade has an agenda. He has to make it up to Ben for treating him so badly – not that Ben will ever know why he acted like he did. Seeing him every day only heightens Wade's regret. If he'd had more courage back then, maybe he and Ben could have been something.

The least he can do is show Ben he's changed.
There's no way Wade can get what he *really* wants – Ben's heart.

OTHER TITLES

Learning to Love
Michael & Sean
Evan & Daniel
Josh & Chris
Final Exam

Sensual Bonds
A Bond of Three
A Bond of Truth

Merrychurch Mysteries
Truth Will Out
Roots of Evil
A Novel Murder

Love, Unexpected
Debt
Burden

Dreamspun Desires
The Senator's Secret
Out of the Shadows
My Fair Brady
Under The Covers

Lions & Tigers & Bears
A Growl, a Roar, and a Purr

Love Lessons Learned
First

Waiting for You
Step by Step
Bromantically Yours
BFF

Collars & Cuffs
An Unlocked Heart
Trusting Thomas
Someone to Keep Me (K.C. Wells & Parker Williams)
A Dance with Domination
Damian's Discipline (K.C. Wells & Parker Williams)
Make Me Soar
Dom of Ages (K.C. Wells & Parker Williams)
Endings and Beginnings (K.C. Wells & Parker Williams)

Secrets – with Parker Williams
Before You Break
An Unlocked Mind
Threepeat
On the Same Page

Personal
Making it Personal
Personal Changes
More than Personal
Personal Secrets
Strictly Personal
Personal Challenges

Personal – The Complete Series

Confetti, Cake & Confessions

Connections
Saving Jason
A Christmas Promise
The Law of Miracles
My Christmas Spirit
A Guy for Christmas

Island Tales
Waiting for a Prince
September's Tide
Submitting to the Darkness

A Material World
Lace
Satin
Silk
Denim

Lightning Tales
Teach Me
Trust Me
See Me
Love Me

Southern Boys
Truth & Betrayal
Pride & Protection
Desire & Denial

Maine Men
Finn's Fantasy
Ben's Boss

Kel's Keeper
Here For You
Sexting The Boss
Gay on a Train
Sunshine & Shadows
Watch and Learn
My Best Friend's Brother

Double or Nothing
Back from the Edge
Switching it up
Out for You
State of Mind

Anthologies

Fifty Gays of Shade
Winning Will's Heart

Come, Play
Watch and Learn

Writing as Tantalus
Damon & Pete: Playing with Fire

ABOUT THE AUTHOR

K.C. Wells lives on an island off the south coast of the UK, surrounded by natural beauty. She writes about men who love men, and can't even contemplate a life that doesn't include writing.

The rainbow rose tattoo on her back with the words 'Love is Love' and 'Love Wins' is her way of hoisting a flag. She plans to be writing about men in love - be it sweet and slow, hot or kinky - for a long while to come.

9 781913 843274